Deadlines:
Murder and Mayhem on the California Coast

Volume #2

I0556356

Central Coast Mystery Writers

Edited by: Susan Tuttle,
Barbara M. Hodges, Marie Marcy

ISBN: 1-941465-17-X
ISBN-13: 978-1941465-17-2

A WriterWithin Publication

Deadlines:
Murder and Mayhem on the California Coast

Volume #2

DEDICATION

This volume is dedicated to the Sisters who began it all:
Sarah Paretsky, Nancy Pickard, Charlotte MacLeod,
Kate Mattes, Betty Francis,
Dorothy Salisbury Davis, and Susan Dunlap

Thanks for making it easier for all women who love to write
and read the mysterious and the arcane.

Deadlines:
Murder and Mayhem on the California Coast

Volume #2

DEDICATION

This volume is dedicated to the Sisters who began it all:
Sarah Paretsky, Nancy Pickard, Charlotte MacLeod,
Kate Mattes, Betty Francis,
Dorothy Salisbury Davis, and Susan Dunlap

Thanks for making it easier for all women who love to write
and read the mysterious and the arcane.

CONTENTS

FOREWORD

Just a few thoughts you might find interesting before you begin reading.

All the writers contained herein are members of the Central Coast Chapter of Sisters in Crime (SinC), a national organization that promotes mystery writers. We run the gamut of sub-genres: cozy, hard-boiled, detective, police procedural, Private Investigator, even paranormal and satire. If we can put a mystery in it to solve, we can write it.

We chose the title of this anthology, "Deadlines", for three reasons. As writers, we are always under one deadline or another in either finishing a story or editing it for print. It's also the name of our Chapter Newsletter. And it's a fun play on words, since we specialize in making all sorts of things dead—on paper, that is.

Putting together an anthology like this is a labor of love; love on the part of those who write stories for it, and love on the part of those who do the work of collecting and editing the stories and formatting the volume that you hold in your hands. It's a lot of work for everyone involved. Luckily, it's work we all love to do.

This particular labor of love was made both easier and harder because of the amazing group of mystery writers who submitted stories. Easy, because there was so little for the three editors to do: a little tweaking here, a suggestion or two there. But also hard because all the stories were phenomenal. It was impossible to turn any of them down.

What is it about the California Coast that inspires mystery? Believe me, when it comes to murder and mayhem, the California Coast is the perfect place to commit both! As you can see in these stories, there's no shortage of inspiration: the ocean, dunes, and hills; the history; the people, birds, and animals; the weather, the traffic, even the shopping.

We've mixed the stories up for you, some nice and long, some short flash fiction and some in-between, just for variety and the fun of reading. That's the best thing about an anthology; if you've a little time, you can read an entire story in five or ten minutes and get full satisfaction. When more leisure rolls around, you can immerse yourself in the longer pieces, wallow in their atmosphere for a more extended period, and still have the satisfaction of finishing the story before daily life once again intrudes on this fictional world.

Best of all, at the end we've listed ways to get in touch with these authors, so you can let them know you enjoyed their stories, follow their blogs and/or, sign up for notices of future releases, find their current books, post reviews, and more.

Now you've reached another Deadline: it's time to sit back, turn the page, and enjoy a little Murder and Mayhem on the California Coast!

Your Editors,
Susan Tuttle
Barbara M. Hodges
Marie Marcy

DIANE BROYLES

Diane Broyles worked for ten years as a writing consultant in the field of marketing communications and several years as an editor. She has written journal and newsletter articles that have been translated and published in French and German. For nine years, she chaired a critique group of fiction writers and is currently active in a small line-editing group for mystery writers.

Diane Broyles wrote A Concrete Solution after she learned Catholic priests must honor the seal of the confessional—even if a person's life is in jeopardy. Father McNulty's name endured many changes. Each time Diane chose a new one, she learned a father with the same name was serving in a local church.

A CONCRETE SOLUTION
by
Diane Broyles

Father McNulty leaned forward in the Mission San Luis Obispo de Tolosa confessional to hear his second confession of the day. He gave no indication he recognized the voice of Scooter Dougherty coming through the darkened window, asking for the father's blessing. Scooter added, "You told me to pray I'd find a job, Father, and now I got me a good one and I want to thank you."

"You must thank the good Lord, too," the father said.

"I just landed a contract to build a three-story parking structure in town. I was real smart when I underbid the other guys with a quote for using expired cement."

"Congratulations . . . but is this legal?"

"I can't worry about that, Father. I have a wife and three kids to feed."

"But won't the structure be unstable?"

"Maybe so, but we'll be gone out of town before anything happens. I have a sister in Detroit." He paused. "You ain't allowed to tell anybody what I say in my confession, right? Just forgive me for my sin."

"Where are you building this parking structure?"

"Over on Nipomo Street, behind Wells Fargo bank. Why?"

"Just curious," the father said. "And you're right. I must honor the seal of the confessional. But I can't forgive you unless you're sorry for your sin."

"Yeah, yeah. Just tell me what prayers I have to say to be forgiven."

"First, you must make right what you've done. Then come back for forgiveness."

"No way, Father. The city manager'll give the contract to that butthead Billy Foster. I'll just say an Act of Contrition and God will forgive me. Maybe I'll throw in a couple of Hail Marys."

"I'm afraid it doesn't work that way. Do you understand?"

"Yeah, yeah. Thanks, Father."

* * *

When Father McNulty had heard all the confessions for the day, he rushed to his computer to learn what could happen if a structure were built of cement with expiration dates that had passed. To his horror, he read about lives lost in Sri Lanka when homes constructed of expired cement collapsed and crushed their occupants.

What can I do? he wondered. *If I say nothing, the people in my city could be killed in a cave-in. But if I violate the seal of the confessional by telling the city manager, I'll be excommunicated from the church. Serving God is my life's passion. I have to find a way to save the people of San Luis Obispo and also protect my calling.*

* * *

Father McNulty spent many sleepless nights pondering a solution to his problem. He prayed harder than he'd ever prayed, but work began on the Nipomo project anyway and it progressed quickly.

One day, the father walked past the construction site, sad to see concrete had already been poured for the first level. Tim, one of his parishioners working at the site, stopped him and shouted, "My wife and I thank you, Father. We heard you prayed that we'd get this contract. We were about to go on welfare." He turned to his coworkers. "Hey, guys. This is the priest who made all this happen!"

The men shouted and waved their hands in thanks.

"My wife told me to invite you for dinner tomorrow," Tim said. "You gotta come."

Father McNulty felt the blood rise to his cheeks as guilt overcame him for doing nothing to stop the inevitable collapse of this structure. But what reason could he give Tim for declining his invitation? "Uh . . . um . . . yes," he said. "I'll be there."

Father McNulty ate little and said less at the dinner the next night as Tim and his wife showered him with thanks. On the walk home, he once more pondered the tragic fate of his people.

As he walked toward the mission and through the garden, he noticed water flowing from a flower bed and onto the sidewalk.

Good heavens, he thought. *We shouldn't be wasting water during the current drought. I need a way to stop this.*

He circled the flower bed and stooped to inspect the runoff. After a moment, he stood. *I have an idea!*

* * *

The next day, Father McNulty approached Tim at the construction site. "Say, Tim, I need to stop the sprinkler water at the mission from running onto the sidewalk. All my solutions are too expensive for the small amount of cash we have in the coffers. You're a creative man. Have you any suggestions?"

Tim stopped working and leaned on his shovel. "That's a tough one, Father. Give me a day to think about it."

"Thanks, Tim. I look forward to hearing from you."

The next morning, Father McNulty was walking down the mission sidewalk, about to snip some daisies, when he saw Tim unloading a wheelbarrow, two sets of tools, a bag of cement and another of sand. The father smiled to himself and waved.

"Hi, Father! Look what I got. I thought you and me could build a curb around the flower bed."

"An excellent idea, Tim. I hope we can afford all this."

"Don't worry, Father. The manufacturer sent us more cement than we ordered. I asked my boss and he said I could donate a bag to the mission."

Tim was about to tear open the bag when Father McNulty stopped him, scissors in hand. "Here, let me help," he said, making a neat cut across the top of the bag.

"Neatness doesn't count when mixing concrete," Tim said, "but it's your party."

Father McNulty enjoyed getting his hands dirty as they spent the day mixing cement with sand and pouring concrete. When done, Tim stepped back to admire their work.

"Great job, Father," he said. "You may have missed your calling."

Father McNulty helped Tim gather his tools and load them and the wheelbarrow into his truck.

* * *

Monday morning, Father McNulty appeared at the front desk of the city manager's office with an empty cement bag under his arm. He was directed into the office where Manager Harry Silvers welcomed him and offered him a chair.

"What can I do for you today, Father?" he asked, sitting down. "And what's that under your arm?"

"I have an empty cement bag and a recommendation for a team of excellent construction workers."

Harry's face showed concern. "You're a little late, Father. We hired a hardworking crew for the Nipomo project and they're well into construction of a parking structure."

"Those are the men I mean," Father McNulty said. "They're good, reliable workers, but the parking structure must be torn down immediately. The men must be put on another job."

Harry looked at him as if he were crazy. "I know you have a direct line to God, Father, but why should we waste the city's money by tearing down what we're in the midst of building? The taxpayers would be furious."

"Better furious than dead," the father said.

Harry sat up. "Dead?"

"And we need to do it soon." Father McNulty handed him the empty bag. "This is a cement bag from the Nipomo construction site. The cement was some extra donated to the mission. I was using it to build a curb around a flower bed when I noticed the expiration date on the cement had long passed." He pulled the story of the Sri Lanka collapse from his pocket. "You might want to read this."

Harry inspected the date beneath the neat scissor cut on the bag. Then he read the Sri Lanka story, his cheeks turning crimson with anger. He closed his eyes and his red face turned so pale that Father McNulty called for some water.

Harry opened his eyes and downed the water. He wiped his mouth and shouted to his assistant, "Marty, get Scooter Dougherty on the line!"

Father McNulty heaved a sigh of relief. *God works in mysterious ways*, he thought, *but sometimes He needs a little help*.

KRISTA LYNN

I'm a late-comer to the author world with a long academic career in earth sciences in my wake instead of years of fiction writing. But, wind is filling my sails this year with the release of Blood Stones: The Haunting of Sunset Canyon, a romantic suspense. Mystery and magic were part of my youth where, on an Arizona gold mine where we grew up, my brothers and I scared each other with an old Ouija Board for entertainment.

My offering in this anthology is Blue Moon Blues, where mysteries are solved by the arcane skills of a sixty-something psychic. Go figure—she often uses her Ouija Board.

Blue Moon Blues
by
Krista Lynn

The signs were all there. Nora Pigeon saw them. Plain as the duplicitous smile on a politician's face. Surely she wasn't the only one who could see that something was wrong.

Her neighbor, Cassandra Cartwright (Cassie to her friends), was a very rich, self-made woman. Her family was a dreary hoard of deadbeats whose members suddenly started buzzing around six weeks ago, after Cassie had what the doctor thought was a mild stroke. Relatives she hadn't heard from for an age were *visiting* to see if she "needed anything". Curious, if not downright suspicious in Nora's opinion. And she was worried that her friend, once sharp as an Oscar Wilde witticism, was now slow of speech and oddly disinterested in her surroundings.

Two things had happened that sent packing any doubts that something untoward was going on in the mansion next door. One, the now solicitous family had hired a new nurse for her, who seemed to do little actual nursing. And two, Brenda, the redheaded niece that Cassie always referred to as headstrong, possessing a sharp tongue and quick temper, had tried to talk her great aunt into making a Living Will. If it wasn't for Angeline, the *Good Niece*, it would seem, Cassie could have changed her Will while her lawyer, John Carlyle, was preoccupied with some sort of security breach in his office. Fortunately, Angeline called Nora and asked her to talk to Cassie, and have her wait for Mr. Carlyle. Nora complied, of course, and the lawyer brought a copy of the Will and convinced Cassie that the original document met with her wishes just fine.

After that, Nora had been allowed to see Cassie once, and talk only twice by phone.

Well, for heaven's sake. There might as well have been a red arrow suspended over the Cartwright house, pointing down at it with the caption: "Criminals at Work Here"!

Nora walked to the big window in her sitting room and looked through the lovely wrought-iron fence into Cassie's side garden. She was curious to see which relatives would show up this evening. Nora guessed because Cassie hadn't bought a ticket on the Pearly Gates Express, the visitors now only numbered three: two great-nieces, Angeline and Brenda, and their Uncle Trevor, Cassie's sister's son. Somehow, that didn't make Nora feel any better. There was something wrong with that threesome.

Nora realized that not everyone appreciated her gift —her psychic abilities—but she at least expected her nephew, Ventura County Sheriff's Detective, Thomas Pigeon, to show more concern about her suspicions of nefarious activity next door. It had been a week since she'd taken a packet of evidence to him at the Sheriff's substation. It contained the name of the nurse and a picture of said nurse with Uncle Trevor, along with photos of the two nieces and a lengthy note explaining her concerns. What if the nurse had a record? Did nephew Tommy follow up on her other suggestions in the note? What was taking him so long to get back to her with some helpful information? It hadn't been easy crouching down behind the shrubbery to get those pictures.

Nora sighed and thought about the many pleasant evenings she'd shared with her neighbor, drinking Cosmos, laying out the Tarot Cards, and tripping over the two Great Danes, Odin and Thor. Nora loved having the dogs around. They were real characters, just like their caretaker, Ms. Cassandra Cartwright, the popular author of racy vampire romance stories. As such, she was an engaging friend and an interesting subject for Nora's readings.

When they got together, Nora always kept the subject of the readings light. Cassie didn't realize just how much Nora often withheld. Before Cassie's stroke, Nora saw signs in the cards that something was coming into her friend's life and it wasn't positive. She had cautioned her to take better care of her health, not work so hard. Nora now saw that the cards' positions on the table weren't just indications of overwork and fatigue that could lead to ill health, but possibly signs of greater danger. Now, with the latest developments next door, Nora's worry quotient was climbing rapidly.

Movement to the right caught Nora's eye. She saw two cars at the gate. She picked up her opera glasses and trained them to the driveway. Angeline, who had been spending a great deal time with her great aunt since she'd become ill, had left earlier and now she was back in her modest Toyota Corolla. Right behind her, Brenda, her cousin with the attitude, in her Mercedes. Brenda was crowding up close, tapping her horn. Attitude, all right. The two girls' uncle had already been there and left. Nora saw him arrive earlier driving Cassie's pearly-white Range Rover. He'd entered the house with a small toolbox. In his expensive slacks and sweater, he didn't look to Nora like the handyman type. He'd left about an hour later, the toolbox in one hand, a duffel bag in the other. He pulled out just a few minutes before the girls showed up.

From this distance Nora couldn't be sure, again cursing her puny-powered binoculars, but she thought she saw Angeline look back at her cousin with an aggravated flip of her hand. There was friction there between blond and redhead. It would be comical under different circumstances.

Well, tonight, Nora was going to do something about the situation. She was going to *read the signs* to help reveal the true nature of Cassie's relatives and their sudden fawning attentions. Tonight was the usual time for their monthly *drinks and dabbling* as Cassie always called it.

"Pour the drinks, Nora, and let's dabble in those *Dark Arts!*" she would say, then laugh and rub her hands together with amusement and anticipation. Yes, tonight, Nora Pigeon wouldn't be turned away. She was going to help her friend tonight—because tonight, she was going in the back door.

When the cars had passed through the gate, Nora walked over to the phone and called her nephew. She had to know if he had found out anything. After about a dozen rings someone finally picked up. "Well, there you are, Tommy, I really need..."

"Uh, ma'am, you must have the wrong number. This is the Sheriff's Department."

"Well, of course it is. I need to talk to my nephew."

"Well, who is your nephew, ma'am?"

"He's a detective. Detective Thomas Pigeon. I thought this was his direct number."

A low chuckle. "Yes, ma'am, it's his desk phone, but he isn't here. Can I take a message?"

"Oh, this isn't his direct cell phone number?"

"No, ma'am."

"Okay, then give me that number, please."

"Well, I can't provide that, but can take a message and he'll get back to you. Is this concerning an ongoing case?"

"Well, it will be a *goings-on case* if I can't talk to him right away." Nora paused to take a deep breath. "This is his aunt, so of course he would give the number to me. So, can you just give me that number, please?" The sound in the receiver changed to a muffle as if someone put a hand over it. Then she could hear the man laughing.

"It's for you, Tom-meee. It's your Auntie Sherlock." The playful sarcasm was unmistakable.

"Okay, Alan, give it here and shut the hell up, all right?"

Another rude chuckle, then a thump, and "Hey, watch it, Pidge!"

Grappling noises and then, "Uh, hello? Aunt Nora?"

"Hello Tommy, dear," she said with a loud sigh "What in heaven's name is going on there? That man wouldn't give me your number." She huffed. "And what did he call me?"

"Um, I don't know. I didn't hear him," he said and hurried to change the subject. "You do have my number. I put it in the address book on *your* cell phone. Remember?"

"Oh, that's right. You know I don't know how to use all the functions on that thing. It's too complicated and besides the electrical wavelengths interfere with my *other* reception," Nora stated, enjoying the loud sigh on the other end of the line and the eye-rolling that no doubt accompanied it. "Now, I hope you got my note and will follow up. And what have you been able to find out about that nurse, Lisa Bradford—if that's really her name. Something foul is afoot over there, and..."

"I did," he interrupted. "I checked with the company that placed her there. All her credentials seem to be in place."

He used his *I've got it handled* tone of voice that always put Nora's teeth on edge.

"Well, of course they would be. And? The rest of your investigation?"

"That's about it, Aunt Nora. The woman's on file with the state as a Licensed Vocational Nurse. She has a home address that checked out."

"Well, what about her past? What did you dig up? She's from eastern Canada. Quebec, I suspect. Definite accent."

"Okay, but that hardly makes anyone a criminal."

"No, but hiring a nurse that seems to only be allowed to do clerical work is rather unusual. And Cassie always typed her own manuscripts."

Thomas cleared his throat. "Unusual, perhaps, but still not criminal. And before you ask, I have a call into the lawyer and did as you suggested in your cryptic note." Then his voice took on a lighter tone, "So, hey, not to worry about your neighbor. I'm sure in no time she'll be writing the next "Full Twilight Moon" or whatever those bloodsucker books are called," he said, chuckling.

Good try Thomas, Nora thought. Nice attempt to divert her attention elsewhere by showing his addled aunt he had been listening when she blathered on about her neighbor. Well, she'd play along.

"Thomas. She is not the author of the *Twilight* books. She writes mature, *serious* bloodsucker books. With sex. Well, actually she finished with vampires because of the argument with her publisher." Nora could hear faint sounds as if someone was shuffling papers.

Now he wasn't even listening. She didn't let it bother her. She picked up her opera glasses, focused on Cassie's house, and continued, "Yes, they had a complete falling out because her publisher insisted she start a message-board, or blog, or whatever, to answer questions from silly readers who wanted to 'know more details about the sexy vampire's paranormal, testosterone-laden desires'."

That got his attention. He cleared his throat. "Ah, well, I can see where that would be a problem, all right."

Nora smiled to herself and continued to watch the house. "She found another publisher. She's writing a whole different series now. You might like this one, Thomas. It's about a sexy, modern-day woman, an FBI agent who is really a chimera who shape-shifts into a she-wolf, with color-changing scales like a trout—when she is not holding court as the beautiful Countess Wolfenbane from St. Petersburg, that is."

"You've got to be kidding. Isn't Cassie Cartwright really old? Where does she come up with this stuff?" Nora pulled the handset away from her ear, looked at it, frowned and put it back to her ear. The arrogance of youth, she thought. She was only five years younger than Cassie!

She closed her glasses with a snap. "It's called Urban Fantasy, and I'll have you know, young man, that Cassie, at seventy-two years of age, is wildly successful at it."

She sighed. She'd done her best with the local authorities. Squaring her shoulders, she said, "I've got to go, dear. I have to prepare. Now, don't forget. The lawyer is *key* in this situation."

"Wait. What do you mean? Aunt Nora, I know you. What's up? Please tell me you aren't going to use the...that board, are you? Remember what happened last time?"

"Of course I remember. The truth was revealed, if memory serves."

"What happened was," he stammered around for the right words, then blurted, "what *always* happens with you and the Ouija—something crazy that interferes with a police investigation!"

"Oh, so you are investigating. Good."

"Uh! Nothing conclusive. Let's just say that you don't need to go over with that Ouija Board."

"Now, don't worry, Tommy. I'll have answers that *will* be conclusive. You just continue with your little police work. We'll compare notes later." And she hung up.

She'd swear she could hear *his* teeth grinding from ten blocks away. She grimaced. She really loved that boy and didn't want to make him worry. But sometimes he needed a little help to see the signs.

Moments later, Nora stood before her round, mahogany *Divining Table*. Tarot Cards were spread out in a pattern she'd designed many years ago. The cards had remained untouched, in the same position since her last reading for Cassie. One card on the table hadn't been turned over that evening. As she remembered, Cassie got a call from her editor with changes that had to be done immediately to meet the release date of her next book. That had distracted Cassie and the energy needed for the reading was lost, so Nora walked Cassie and her two four-legged boys to the friendship gate and said goodnight.

Two days later, Cassie fainted after taking Odin and Thor for a walk, which was really more like driving a buckboard across a rough prairie. It would have exhausted a much younger person. Her housekeeper heard strange moaning howls from the back yard and found Cassie lying on the steps—both dogs standing over her. Two days after that, the relatives showed up.

Pulling her thoughts back to the Divining Table, Nora looked at the cards and frowned. The Seven of Swords card had bothered her at the time of the reading because it indicated betrayal and theft. But it was in the reverse position, upside down on the table, so Nora had translated it as Cassie's innate independence about her writing career. Now, she saw its veiled warning.

Nora took a deep breath and said aloud, "Show me in a way I can understand." After several minutes of meditative study of the cards as a whole, she turned over the last one. She sighed. A reverse Queen of Cups. "Oh, Cassie dear. I am so sorry about this dark-haired girl who is going to break your heart."

Nora fumbled with her cell phone, clicking several times until she found the Contacts and punched the only one listed: her nephew. A minute later she'd given him a new instruction, took a turn at rolling *her* eyes, then reached beside the Divining Table along the wall and grabbed a large, leather folio case. Inside was her most treasure possession, a very old Ouija Board.

She went out her back door and slipped through the friendship gate that linked her garden with Cassie's. As she walked in through the service porch at the rear of the house, both dogs looked up from their naps and thumped their tails with desultory zeal. Some watch dogs, they were practically comatose. Nora stumbled as she tried to get through the obstacle course their prone bodies made. She noticed a large can of flea powder. The lid was lying next to it. Hmm. She looked at the dogs, and frowned.

She continued through the kitchen and down a hallway. As she passed a small sitting room, Nora glanced in and stopped. Cassie was sitting in her chair in front of the bay window with a blanket over her lap. Nora smiled. She had shared this room many times with her friend. The window overlooked a rose garden and through the trees, with the small city of Ventura below, Nora saw a picturesque seascape that glowed in the setting sun. She knew that later in the evening, the scene would look like a bed of diamonds under a full moon. In fact, a rare Blue Moon with strong celestial energy that Nora was sure would help her efforts this evening. As she stepped closer she realized Cassie's head was tilted to the side as if she were asleep.

"Cassie, dear," Nora said and touched her friend's shoulder. No immediate response. Nora added a little more pressure and was relieved when Cassie's eyes opened. "Cassie, it's me, Nora."

A blank stare for a moment, then, "Nora! How delightful. When did you get here?"

When Nora reached out and took Cassie's hands, she was dismayed at the signs of illness on her friend's face. "I've just arrived."

"Oh, well, then," Cassie said, flustered. "Please, have a seat. I'll see if, um, *someone* is around to bring some more tea. I . . ." She looked at Nora and shook her head as if to clear her thoughts. "I was just having some myself and must have dozed off."

Nora pulled a side chair closer, propped the Ouija Board case next to it and, once seated, reached over and picked up the teapot. She took off the lid and smelled the now cold contents. "Hmm. This is different. What kind of tea is it?"

"Oh, I'm not sure of the name. It has a distinctive smell, doesn't it? It's actually very strong compared to what I usually drink. I believe one of the girls told me it is an Earl Grey with lavender or some other flower?" Cassie said and craned her neck to look toward the door, then glanced back to the end table next to her. "Where is my bell?"

"That's okay, dear," Nora said as she picked up the teapot. "I'll take this and your cup and brew us a fresh pot. Be right back."

A few steps from the kitchen doorway, Nora heard two female voices. She stopped and listened. She'd only met Angeline one time. From her position she couldn't see the young women and their voices sounded similar—a definite handicap to effective eavesdropping. She couldn't be sure which young woman was talking.

"So what if she's a nurse. She can type like the wind and can transcribe Aunt Cassandra's next She-Wolf Sisterhood book from her tapes and then lickety-split, it's off to the publisher before . . ."

"Before what?"

"Well, while she's still able to, uh, handle whatever an author does—sign contracts, make edits—whatever."

"You are unbelievable. Lisa Bradford is a skilled homecare *nurse*. She should be taking care of Aunt Cassandra's *person*, not her writing career just so there'll be more royalties to enjoy—after she's gone!"

"Oh, shut your mouth. I'm here just as much as you are to take care of her, you know."

"Yeah, you and Uncle Trevor are just taking care of yourselves, is what you're doing. I saw him in town on the way out here driving Aunt Cassandra's Range Rover. And is it true Aunt Cass gave him the keys to her condo in Redondo Beach?"

"Who told you that?"

"Lisa. She also said Uncle Trevor has been "fixing" things in the garage and around the house." A derisive laugh before she continued. "Uncle Trevor? Who can't fix a broken shoelace?"

"What is *Nurse Lisa* now? Your spy? And how the hell do I know what he's doing? I'm sure he's just trying to help out. He and Auntie are close, you know."

"Well, I think asking for her condo is inappropriate."

"Why are you acting so high and mighty? You're just trying to get up the nerve to ask for an extension on your considerable *Auntie Cassandra* funded loan."

"That's a loan, not a hand-out. You two are freeloading here, and you know it."

"Oh, you are such a bitch. I don't have to listen to this!"

"Well, go then."

"No, you go!"

An impatient groan-enhanced sigh, then a sound like a cabinet door being slammed. It was an effective punctuation to the end of the conversation, followed by a lingering ellipsis of silence, leaving Nora to wonder what she was missing.

After a few moments, Nora took the cue to step into the kitchen and found Brenda, her stance rigid, arms folded like two steel straps in front of her. She was glaring at a doorway that led into the dining room. Nora wondered, frustrated, which girl had said what.

When Brenda noticed Nora, her arms snapped to her sides. "What are you doing here? How did you get in?"

"I came in through the friendship gate that links our two gardens. Cassie and I often get together on Thursday evenings."

Brenda looked at the teapot and cup in Nora's hand, then back at Nora with raised eyebrows.

"Your aunt is in the sitting room by the back service area. I'm here to get another pot of tea. I thought I'd just wash this one out," Nora said. "This is a rather strange smelling tea. Very pungent. Cassie says she'd never had it until her illness." She held the teapot out. "Are you familiar with this tea?"

Brenda trained her gaze on Nora's face for several seconds, then ignoring the teapot she asked, "You're her friend that reads the Tarot, aren't you? You're a psychic, or so Aunt Cassandra believes."

"Yes. I'm Nora Pigeon. Cassandra and I have been friends for a long time," Nora answered and headed for the sink, noting Brenda's skeptical scowl.

"I believe you have recently influenced my aunt about . . . personal matters."

Nora figured Brenda referred to the Living Will episode. She rinsed the teapot and set it aside and turned to her. "I think your aunt is not easily influenced by anyone. She is quite capable of knowing her own mind," Nora said as she washed and dried the cup. She set it beside the pot then turned to Brenda and added, "When she is allowed to."

Brenda stared for a second as if sorting out the meaning behind Nora's words. Her gaze strayed to the doorway to the dining room. "I'm sure I don't know what your mean."

"Well, she's been ill, and perhaps has felt she needed to defer to others." Again, the younger woman took her time to form a comment, so Nora walked over to a copper canister on the counter, reached in and pulled out two Lipton tea bags. She put them in the pot and proceeded to fill it with scalding water from the boiling-water dispenser at the sink.

"You seem to know your way around here."

Nora got a tray out from a lower cabinet and placed the pot and two clean cups and saucers on it. "I've spent many happy hours here with your Great Aunt, and likewise, she and the *Boys* at my house as well," she said with a smile at the reference to Odin and Thor. "Speaking of the big guys, they seemed to be feeling under the weather when I saw them on the service porch. Perhaps they need a vet check."

"What? The dogs?"

"They are not their usual selves. They're lethargic poor dears, not unlike their mistress."

Brenda shook her head and huffed out a sigh. "Okay, I know you and auntie are close, but that doesn't give you a right to meddle in family business. And from now on, until Aunt Cassandra is better, please let us know you are coming to visit," Brenda said, her tone curt. "I know she must be glad of company, but auntie needs her rest, so please don't draw out your stay this evening."

With that, Brenda turned and left the room.

Nora carried the tea-laden tray back to the sitting room. Cassie turned from the window with a tired smile. "Oh, how nice, Nora," she said then pointed to the end table next to the sofa. "And there are shortbread cookies in that drawer."

Nora set the tray on the table and after securing two cookies each, poured the tea and settled into her chair. "Cassie dear, I have two questions for you."

"Yes, of course. Go ahead."

"Would you like to *dabble* this evening? If you're up to it, that is."

"Yes! Oh yes, I would really like that. It would definitely do me good." She paused and looked at her friend, expectantly. "What is the other question?"

Nora leaned in a little closer and asked, "Do your nieces color their hair?"

Cassandra tilted her head then said with a laugh, "Maybe both." She squinted her eyes. "Okay, tell me what you are thinking, Nora Pigeon."

Nora took a deep breath. "I'm thinking you haven't been yourself. You should have recuperated from a *mild stroke* weeks ago. I'm thinking we need to find out why you haven't."

Minutes later, the nieces appeared at the door from different directions, bumping into and glaring at each other. They pushed into the room then stopped with hands on hips, lips pursed tight as like zippered handbags. Except for their different hair color, they could have been twins. Before they could unzipper and speak, Cassie informed them they were to join her and Nora in the dining room.

By the time Cassie had made known that everyone in the house should humor her and join in on the *Dabbling* fun, it was almost eight o'clock. Nora took a moment to gaze out the large picture window. The night was aglow in moonlight. She felt the energy of this second moon in the month, knowing that a Blue Moon would shed more than lunar illumination on the evening. It would shed light on Cassie's situation, she thought as she turned to watch Nurse Lisa who was setting up the gaming table and bringing in more chairs. Nora noticed the woman's furtive demeanor and the pallor of her face. The nieces were not pleased—their faces were quite colored with irritation. The moon's influence was already at work.

When Angeline said with a huff that she'd be right back and Brenda followed her out with the same promise thrown over her shoulder, Nora took the opportunity to pull out her Ouija Board.

Cassie looked surprised when Nora started to remove it from the case. "Why, Nora, that's your *Talking Board*. You rarely use it, except when you're helping your nephew..." Her voice trailed off, and her eyes widened at Nora who returned her gaze with a slight nod of her head.

"Are you really up for this?" Nora asked.

After a few seconds, Casandra Cartwright sat up straighter and nodded. "I believe I am."

When the two nieces came back in, Lisa was finishing the lighting of the candles as Cassie instructed. Brenda looked surprised and curious at the ambiance of the setting, Nora noted. Nora also registered the level of sarcasm in Angeline's voice when she said, "Oh, for heaven's sake. Let's get this little séance, or whatever it is, over with, shall we? You've already lighted the candles. Oooh, the mood is set. So, what do we do now?"

Brenda took a seat. "You seem nervous, Angie. What's wrong? Afraid of what might be *revealed*?"

Angeline gave her cousin a sharp look, pulled out a chair opposite and sat down. "If I was you, I'd be more afraid of your *own* secrets, cousin dear."

Nora dimmed the lights, momentarily dampening the palpable animosity between Brenda and Angeline. In the candle glow, for the first few heartbeats as each woman looked at the Ouija, their faces revealed many things to Nora. With a hushed tone, she told them to remain as quiet as possible, focus on the board and place their fingertips on the planchette. "Keep the pressure light," she told them, "but don't break contact with it."

"But isn't this Ouija Board really supposed to be for contacting dead spirits? Who do we need to contact?"

"Well, yes, Brenda, the first use of the *Talking Board* was as a medium to do just that. However, this Ouija is very old and has historically been used to contact the real spirit, the character, if you will, of the people who sit around it. Sort of what is really in their hearts. We can ask it questions and it will answer truthfully."

"Oh brother," Angeline said rolling her eyes. She added her fingertips on the heart shaped planchette with Nora's and Cassie's, and after a brief pause, Brenda added hers. Lisa was reluctant, her eyes transfixed on the board. Wary.

Cassie encouraged her by saying that it was okay. "It's all in fun, right, Nora?"

"Well, it can be very entertaining," Nora responded. When Lisa finally touched the planchette, Nora looked into her eyes and smiled. Lisa smiled back, a shy smile of connection if not one of complete trust.

Then, for the next ten minutes, it was interesting, if not amusing, as the two nieces sniped back and forth. They took turns asking questions that demeaned each other's character, and then moved the planchette to the desired answer to irritate the other. Finally, Cassie cleared her throat and said she had a question.

"Where is Uncle Trevor?" Everyone looked at her and then at the board.

"Focus, and keep contact, everyone," Nora said. Several long seconds went by, and just before patience ran out, the planchette started to move downward and stopped at the words, "Good Bye". Angeline scoffed, under her breath.

"Goodbye? Does that mean he left? When, then, will he be back?" she asked with a note of disdain, but watched intently as it moved to the word, "NO".

"I asked when," she said, tartly, and kept staring hard at the planchette until it moved slightly to the left, and then snapped back on "NO". She put her hands on her hips and looked around the table, "Well, what does that mean?"

Nora asked her to put her hand back in place, and as soon as she did, the planchette quickly spelled out "G-O-N-E".

"What? Okay, who is moving this damned thing?" Angeline demanded.

"Aren't you?" asked Brenda, with a smirk.

Cassie cleared her throat again. With a sigh she asked, "Where did Trevor go?"

The heart-shaped pointer moved to "A-S-K" then moved away from the letters before pointing to "A".

Angeline huffed out a breath. "O-kay, then, 'Ask a . . .' what?"

"I think that's 'Ask A'—meaning someone with the name starting with 'A', obviously," Brenda said. "And, let's see. Oh, yeah. Your name starts with an 'A'. So where is he?"

"Me? Why would I know where Uncle T is? You're his favorite, Bren. He was here earlier with a toolbox," Angeline continued.

"Trevor *owns* a toolbox?" Cassie asked with a laugh. "Whatever could do with tools with all those thumbs?"

The index fingers of all five hands still rested on the planchette—so it gave an answer. "J-E-W-E-L-S". The nieces gasped and stared at each other. Cassie slumped in her seat.

Lisa's gaze darted from Brenda to Angeline and it seemed to Nora that she wanted to say something.

Nora leaned over and whispered in Lisa's ear. "If you know, now is the time to act." Lisa bit her bottom lip then shook her head.

"What about jewels?" Angeline demanded, her gaze locked on her cousin.

The Ouija obliged again to the work"GOODBYE".

"What the hell?" Angeline hissed, her gaze still trained on Brenda. "What have you been up to?"

"Me?" Brenda fired back. "The Board just said to ask you!"

Nora turned her attention to Cassie who looked even paler than before. "Just wait, dear," she assured her. "All will be fine."

Before the two nieces could continue their confrontation, Nora pressed on in a different direction to keep them off balance. "I have a question. Will Cassie recuperate from her stroke, soon?" Now, everyone looked at Nora and then at Cassie, but their eyes were quickly pulled back to the board when the planchette started to move. It slid back up to "NO", then pointed at the letters: "S-T-R-O-K-E".

Several moments went by as the five women stared at the board. Then Lisa spoke. "I think that was 'No stroke'," she said, putting the response together. All eyes went to her, but she kept her eyes down at the board.

Nora asked the next question. "Then why is Cassie still ill?"

"D-O-G-S"

"What the . . .?" Brenda said, shaking her head.

Again, Nora hastened to ask, "The dogs, Odin and Thor, are making Cassie sick?" the planchette moved to spell, "F-L-E-A-S"

"Oh, for heaven's sake, Aunt Cassie! The dogs' fleas are poison . . . uh, making you sick!" Angeline said. She tried to rally sarcasm, but only managed shaky, edgy. She pushed back her chair and started to get up. A candle on a nearby table was knocked over at the same moment the doorbell rang.

Brenda jumped up and grabbed the candle. "Just where are you going?" she asked Angeline when she started to push past. A loud knock on the front door froze everyone in place. After a few moments, Cassie broke the ice. "Well, someone needs to answer the door." She started to rise but Lisa touched Cassie's arm and got up instead. Brenda moved to stop Angeline's sidestep to exit the room.

Nora had noted all the activity since the Ouija's shocking responses, particularly Brenda and Angeline, who were close to blows. But she was equally interested in Lisa and watched her as she went to the door. Lisa flinched at a second insistent knock followed by a deep voice, "This is the Ventura County Sheriff's Department. Official business."

The young nurse paused, looked down, took a deep breath then opened the door. Nora's nephew, Detective Thomas Pigeon stepped in followed by a Sheriff's Deputy. Thomas looked around then pursed his lips when he saw Nora and the obvious Ouija Board activity. Nora gave him the *don't-be-like-that* look then shifted her gaze to the portly gentleman who came in next. It was Mr. Carlyle, Cassie's attorney. He looked around the room and then raised his arm and pointed at Brenda. "That woman works in my office. She has full access to our scanned document server! I had no idea a *Brenda Foley* was related to Ms. Cartwright."

All eyes trained on Brenda as she fumbled with a response. "I . . . well Foley was my married name—for all of seven months. I haven't had time to change it back. I wasn't trying to hide my relationship with you, Aunt Cassie. I just needed a part-time job until you got well."

"The virus that attacked the server in my office could only come from the computer attached to the scanner. The one you used," said the lawyer.

"What? I didn't have anything to do with that!"

Nora stepped forward. "Mr. Carlyle, what happened? What did the virus do?"

"It messed up the files! The older ones that aren't in *The Cloud*, that is. It re-set all the file dates, changing the last edited dates to the date and time the virus hit. All of them! All the same date!" He stopped and took out his handkerchief, wiped his forehead and looked from Cassie to the detective. "So, no one could tell if someone had opened the file and taken a page out, altered it, or replaced the whole document!"

He swayed, his face red, his neck puffed out over his collar. He took a ragged breath and continued. "It has been a nightmare trying to find which lawyer, associate or paralegal last worked on a specific file so we can have an idea of timeline. I went to *my* associate and she had Cassandra's Will in her files on her desktop, thank heaven. We just happened to check the hard copy in my office to make sure her digital one matched the one I had, and that's when I noticed the changes. That's how I know the original will of Cassandra Cartwright has been altered—on the file server and in the hardcopy I have."

He looked directly at Cassie. "I was asked to bring it here for you to go over, Cassandra. Remember when you wanted to make a Living Will all of a sudden?"

Wiping his forehead, the lawyer finally had to take a seat. "This is a terrible breach, and a felony. You must arrest that girl, Deputy. She is now the sole beneficiary of her aunt's estate!"

"What!?" Brenda cried and then looked at her great-aunt.

Cassie's weak voice punched through the stunned room. "Oh, Brenda."

"No, auntie, I didn't do this."

Thomas stepped over to Brenda. "We'd like you to come down to the station to answer some questions, Mrs. Foley." He looked around the room then gave a quick questioning look at Nora. "The woman who answered the door? Where is she?"

Angeline offered, "Oh, she skedaddled right out when you came in, detective."

"She's wanted in connection with several crimes in upstate New York," Thomas said and nodded to the Deputy who turned and went out the door.

Angeline stepped closer to her aunt and with a confrontational look at her cousin, said, "So, Lisa's in on it with you, huh? That's why you hired her—because she is actually a computer wiz as well as a nurse? Yes, Uncle Trevor knew all about your little *Nurse* Lisa. She's a hacker."

"Well, *I* didn't know. She was the one who showed up for the interview." Brenda appealed to Cassie. "Aunt Cassie I was trying to get someone who would take better care of you. The other nurse didn't even respond when you called for her half the time. Then when Lisa started she was at least worried about you even though Angeline kept her busy doing other things." Brenda whirled back to Angeline. "Uncle Trevor knew Lisa?"

Angeline put her hand on Cassie's shoulder. "Well, let's just say he had his suspicions."

Brenda took a several steps toward Angeline, her hands in fists at her side. "You came to the office to take me to dinner. You said we should try to be friends. When was that, exactly? It was before you started trying to get Aunt Cass to make a Living Will to stir things up. It was YOU! You hacked the server."

Frowning, Detective Pigeon moved between the two women to forestall further escalation of hostilities. Angeline leaned to the side and pointed at her cousin. "She's nuts. I don't know the first thing about making a computer virus."

"But I do."

Everyone turned to look at the open front door. Lisa Bradford stood there with a laptop in one hand and a folio-sized book in the other. Angeline gasped and slapped her hand over her mouth.

Lisa walked over to Nora and handed her the items. "I *do* know—everything they were doing. But they said they'd turn me in. Trevor knows about me. He knows my ex-husband. He said he'd tell him and the authorities where I was. I'm so sorry."

When Nora looked at the computer and book, then to Lisa for explanation, Lisa said, "That's Trevor's computer with the Trojan virus I wrote, and the book . . ." she turned and pointed at Angeline, "is her Notary Public book. She and Trevor forged Ms. Cartwright's name in there. They forged the Quit Deed to a house in Redondo Beach and somehow got the pink slip to the Rover and forged that, too."

"Where did you get my Notary book? I . . . I didn't forge anything!" Angeline looked from her great-aunt to Brenda then bolted from the room, Detective Pigeon hot on her trail. Nora knew she wouldn't get past the dog barricade. Several yelps, and loud bangs, and then screams, as Angeline fought dog limbs and the strong arm of the law for her freedom.

When Detective Pigeon marched Angeline back into the dining room, she had white powder on her face. "Stop!" she yelled. "Let me clean this off my face! It's poison!"

"Don't worry dear," Nora said. "You know organophosphates won't kill you right off, just give you a variety of symptoms. You'll be quite sick for a few hours, a dose of nausea, and muscle weakness, well deserved, I'd say." Nora smiled at the look of shock on Angeline's face. When Nora turned and saw the look of disbelief on Cassie's, she went to her and explained what had been happening and why she was so sick.

"She put extra flea powder on the dogs, and dosed your tea with it. The type of chemical in flea powder can cause lots of symptoms, but will also clear out of your system quickly, so when you went to the doctor with your complaints, you were actually already feeling better. Once you were back home, though, she probably started dosing you again, putting extra powder on the dogs knowing they were your constant companions."

Nora put her arm around her friend's shoulder and asked her if it was Angeline or Brenda who tried to get her to make a Living Will. When she replied that it was Angeline, Nora nodded. "Angeline, you lied to me. You lied to everyone. The whole thing was a ruse to get the lawyer to come over here. And then I helped out by convincing your great-aunt to have the lawyer bring his copy of the will—*somehow*, hers was lost—so you could switch out the new pages." You were the one who loaded the virus onto your cousin's computer to hide the fact that you'd doctored your aunt's will."

"I didn't have anything to do with that. It's those two," she said, pointing at Lisa then Brenda. She squirmed under Thomas' grip. He moved so she could take a handkerchief Cassie had pulled from her pocket.

"Give it up, Angeline," Brenda said. "Quit lying. You just tried to run out of here."

"You're trying to set me up, that's why," Angeline spat back as she furiously wiped at her face. "*You're* the beneficiary, Brenda. Why would Trev . . . uh, why would anyone not put their name on it."

Lisa spoke from behind Nora's shoulder. "I only have what I overheard, but Trevor told Angeline that it was brilliant—the only way to get away with it all—to put Brenda as the beneficiary. That way if it was noticed—the changed Will that is—then Brenda would be blamed and then Ms. Cartwright would be more generous with the two of them."

"Oh, you liar. You shut your damned mouth, or . . ."

"Or what?" Brenda asked with a snort. Angeline's expression appeared blank, glassy, like the troubled, dark-spirited person indicated by the Queen of Cups Tarot card in the reversed position—the dark-haired girl.

"Lisa, what did they say would happen if Brenda inherited as per the altered Will?" Nora asked.

Lisa took a deep breath and raised her eyes to Angeline. "Trevor said they'd take care of her then, too."

Rubbing his forehead, Carlyle cleared his throat. "Oh, god," he moaned. "The *Will* states that in the event of Brenda Foley's death, the beneficiary, the whole estate, goes to Mr. Trevor Cartwright."

"Just him?" Angeline blurted, then clamped her mouth tight.

Cassie put her face in her hands. Nora leaned down. "I'm sorry this has happened to you, dear. But it will all be sorted out, I promise."

"Yeah, well it will be sorted down at the station," Detective Pigeon said as he released Angeline's arm with a stern look that kept her in place so he could take out his cell phone. Everyone started talking/accusing at once at that point, but Nora watched her nephew. His eyes widened as he listened. A moment later he nodded and said, "Okay, good work. Go pick him up."

When he turned and found his aunt staring at him, Thomas shook his head. "How did you know Trevor Cartwright would go down to the Pawn Shop on Thompson

Boulevard? He was there. Pawned a large diamond ring this evening. The owner identified his picture."

"The Seven of Swords, actually. Well, I didn't know for sure who the thief was. Could have just been the Dark Haired Girl, but it became clear during our visit with The Talking Bo . . ."

The Detective put up his hand. "Oh, don't tell me, Aunt Nora. Please don't say anymore."

"Okay, Thomas dear. But I have to add that we owe Lisa Bradford for her honesty." When Thomas frowned but nodded, she asked, "Can you take a statement from Cassie here instead of at the station? She's not well and this has been an awful shock."

"Okay," he replied as he took Angeline's arm again. "I'll just get a few facts. The rest all have to go, including the lawyer. What a family, huh?"

Angeline tried to shake Thomas off so he turned her around and handcuffed her. "Ouch! Why don't you handcuff her," she yelled as she knifed her cousin with a look.

"Brenda is blameless," Nora said directly to Angeline.

Thomas glanced up and acknowledged a man who had just come in. The man saw Nora and began to laugh. Nora squinted her eyes at him and started to ask Thomas if that was his rude partner who wouldn't tell her his direct number, but her nephew cut her off. "So. . . uh, why's she innocent?"

Nora pursed her lips, but answered. "Brenda is a real redhead, whereas this one is not a natural blond."

Thomas took a big breath, glared at his partner who choked back a snort, and asked, "So, this you got from the cards, Aunt Nora?"

"I thought you didn't want me to say," Nora answered with a smile.

Minutes later, all suspects and the lawyer were tucked into two unmarked Detective cars and one Deputy's cruiser. Nora walked out to talk to her nephew. "Thomas, Lisa Bradford needs help."

Thomas looked at her for a second. "She does seem to be in a lot of trouble. I expect she'll be picked up in a couple of days and taken back to Canada."

"I can help her, Thomas, but . . . you know I need something."

With a groan, Thomas walked over to his car and talked to Lisa. In a minute, he walked back and placed something in Nora's hand. "I don't want you to get involved, Aunt Nora, but I know I can't stop you when you set your mind." When Nora gave him a kiss on the cheek, he smiled. "Just keep me in the loop."

She patted him on his arm. "Oh, of course, dear. I always do."

"Yeah, right."

When the cars left, Nora opened her hand. A slim silver chain with a tiny cross sat warmly in the palm of her hand. "This will work quite nicely," Nora said to the diamonds sprinkled under the full glow of a very helpful Blue Moon.

Susan Tuttle

Susan Tuttle is a professional editor, writing teacher and the slightly twisted, award-winning author of the suspense novels *Tangled Webs, Piece By Piece* and *Sins of the Past,* the newly released historical suspense novel, *A Matter of Identity,* the indieB.R.A.G. Medallion-awarded paranormal suspense novel, *Proof of Identity,* a short story collection, *Death in the Valley,* and the comprehensive 6-volume *Write It Right: Exercises to Unlock the Writer in Everyone* workbook series based on her writing classes, for fiction writers of all levels. Her work has also appeared in anthologies for SLO NightWriters and Central Coast Sisters in Crime, in Tolosa Press and various literary journals.

Susan, a past president of SLO NightWriters and the Central Coast Chapter of Sisters in Crime and presently the newsletter editor for both organizations, is hard at work on her paranormal Skylark detective series, and two YA fantasy series.

"Bukra" was written as a class writing assignment. We had 15 minutes and had to use two strange words (bukra and atmus) in such a way that readers could figure out what they meant from the way they were used. This is what I wrote that day.

Bukra

by
Susan Tuttle

Lapis sky, green palms and sand the color of pale gold had never set foot anyplace around here. Not even when dinosaurs roamed the earth and heat had smothered it. This was god's forsaken land, up near the so-called magnetic north, where nothing lived that couldn't survive sub-zero temperatures, yard-thick ice and blinding snowstorms.

Ah, Alaska in December. A frozen hell on earth for most. Paradise for me.

You could get away with pretty much anything up here as long as you knew where to bury the bodies so it would take a few thousand or so years to find them—and if you had an isolated place to hole up in when the weather turned cranky. And I did. Get away with stuff, I mean. Lots of stuff, both legal and un. The un was by far the most satisfying.

I also had a little place out by the Atmu. Natives are scared of Atmus, think their ancestors live inside those craggy hills. Idiots. My nearest neighbor was some twenty miles away as the crow flies, a good 6 or 7 hours by fast-running dogsled. Didn't see anyone for months at a time, but I never got too lonely. When the hunger bit me to the bone, I'd just harness up Pete, Cleaver, Josie and Hush-mush, head on over to the nearest settlement and pick me up a nice juicy companion. Took mebbe three days going the long way, up over the Atmu, across the top of that flat little peak, then down the other side. I dug out the way myself since there weren't no trail to speak of when I moved out there, just slick narrow ledges ending in abrupt thousand-foot drops. But I thought I'd most probably need a hidden access, so I did the work and proved myself right on my first expedition.

Course you gotta be smart about it. No sense hiding out only to get caught when you ventured home. I'd bury my supplies about half a mile from the cabin, remove the wool felt I used to chock all the holes between the rotting boards, and leave the place looking deserted as an old western ghost town. Anyone looking for my latest capture would think the place had been abandoned long ago and ride right on by. Only had to hide out in that cave I found on my side of the Atmu a couple times. Good thing I'd thought ahead and left some provisions in there. Gave me a chance to see if'n I'd picked right or not. Woman who can't cook ain't worth nothing in this life.

All was going well until that last one. Ing'go her name was, though I just called her bitch. Some kind of princess or priestess or whatever these ice land savages call their religious-type leaders. I knew we'd have a while to camp out in that cave on the Atmu, cause her daddy was a real bigwig among the igloos. They'd not give up looking for a long time, probably not 'til I gave 'em reason to. Shoulda done her in the first night, even though she could cook. Wouldn't be where I am had I been smart.

Ing-go surprised me. Didn't cry like all them others. She just looked at me with those weird eyes she had, not dark like all the other tribe-people's, but a kinda deep silvery gray. Caught the firelight a few times that first night just like a cat and scared the be-jeezus outa me, I don't mind admitting. Felt better once I taught her not to look at me anymore.

But she could cook, and did a right fine job with not much persuasion. Rather disappointed me, it's a rush hitting a woman and watching her cringe and grovel. But Ing'go took to instruction with just a few gestures from me and I had a nice filled-up belly every night.

Had to tie her down to sleep, didn't want her running off to daddy the minute I closed my eyes, and she didn't even fight that. She sat nice and quiet, awake when I fell asleep and still sitting there, eyes wide, when I woke up again. Never did see her sleep, though I taught her good how to warm my bed. Man, she could warm the devil's soul, I swear. Anyways, I forgot to tie her one night that second week of hiding out, got flamboozled by her being so quiet-like, but there she was when I jerked upright, heart pounding. Never even tried to get away. Thought she was a bit simple minded, I did. But that didn't matter. It weren't her mind I was interested in.

It was sometime in that second week in the cave that she spoke for the first time.

"Bukra," she said as she offered up my meal from where I taught her, on her knees. She'd say the same thing every time she brought me food or drink. "Bukra." Over and over. I figured it meant "master" or some such. Damn, but I'd picked good this time. Thought maybe I'd keep her a year or two, mebbe more, if her daddy ever stopped looking. He and his men was out there every day and I was getting antsy. Didn't want to hang in this cave too much longer, not with a nice little cabin with a proper bed to chain her to waiting down the valley. But daddy kept on searching, though he steered right clear of that Atmu. Long's we stayed there, weren't no way he was ever gonna find her.

Weren't til around the middle of the third week that I started feeling strange. Heavy. Like a sickness was brewing down in my belly. She'd told me her name by then, and the words for cup, plate, food, drink. And fucking. All life's necessities. She still said, "Bukra" with every meal, giving me that little dip of her head, like a well-trained slave. But when I asked her what it meant, she just gestured to the cave walls and floor and shrugged.

That sickness got hold of me and slowed me down right good. She coulda got away real easy then, but she stayed. I figured it was cause I'd trained her real well by then. One lift of a fist and she was cowering by the wall, stroking her fingers down that dark, cold rock. I moved my bunk across the opening slit, which was so narrow I had trouble getting in and out myself, just so's she couldn't slip by me at night. But Ing'go, she was crafty enough not to try. She had other plans in that pretty little head of hers.

Sometime in the fifth week of hiding I began to hear the noises. A soft whispering at first, more like water dripping somewhere deep in the cave, though I'd explored it and knew it weren't all that deep. And ain't no dripping water anywheres in Alaska in December. Never got truly dark by the Atmu either, not fully. That watery light cast the weirdest shadows on them cave walls. Looked like big cats stalking, then whales smashing their tails onto the ice to break through to the depths. Then the aurora gleamed along the dark stone before winking out into a moment or two of pitch black.

The sounds grew louder and I grew heavier, could hardly lift up my arms or legs. I figured mebbe seven weeks we'd been in that place by then, and her daddy still out there looking. It was making me nuts, seeing stuff from the corner of my eyes, things that weren't never there, and hearing voices whisper almost-words. I grabbed hold of that little piece of tail and shook her til her eyes wobbled in their sockets, trying to get an answer from her. But all she'd say was, "Bukra." Just, "Bukra."

Then she started giving me, well, I don't quite know what to call it. A look that was half smirk, half pity and all calculation. I was standing up by then, trying to get some strength back into my legs, leaning against the rear wall. She reached up on tiptoe, caressed my face, then gave my cheek a kiss. Man, that kiss stung, it was so cold. We'd run out of food about three weeks before and the water was close to gone, though it didn't seem to slow her down none. I knew I had to find the strength to move, to get out of that cave and back to my place, daddy or no daddy. Woulda given up that sweet little piece of tail, too, if I coulda moved. But I couldn't. I watched as Ing'go brought my notebook and pencil from my knapsack. She set 'em on a rock beside me, then smiled.

"Bukra," she said, and gestured to my feet.

I looked down. My heart lurched. My feet were gone! My lower legs, too, they'd become part of that cave wall. I shook my head and looked again. Saw what was happening as the creepies clawed up my spine. The stone wavered as I watched, then it crawled another inch up, touched my knees.

"What the fuck?" I screamed. "You little bitch, what did you do? I'll kill you! Kill you!"

I struggled, but no way could I break the hold that wall had on me. The voices rose around me, human-like now, a sound of anguish and pain and torture. And in the weird light I finally saw them clear, figures encased in the stone around me. Living, breathing, stone people caught forever in a frozen hell.

I looked at Ing'go. She smiled at me, triumph and sorrow both in her eyes.

"Atmu is place of gods," she said. "Bukra is justice."

Then she bowed and walked out. Into the light, the snow, the air. Into freedom. And left me here.

Ain't got much time, now. I'm almost all stone. If'n you find this, look for me in the eerie half-light of December.

Listen for my voice in the not-quite-sounds of the rock. Then seal up this god-forsaken cave and get off the Atmu, lest Bukra snare you, too.

TONY PIAZZA

Tony Piazza is a mystery writer, film historian, and veteran storyteller renowned for his passion for writing and movies. He is the author of four mystery novels and a non-fiction work. Actor and stand-in for movies and television, Piazza has appeared in such notable films as Magnum Force and The Streets of San Francisco. From Clint Eastwood to Steve McQueen, Piazza's stories read like a who's who of Hollywood. He is also a member of Sisters in Crime, Mystery Writers of America and SLO Nightwriters.

Private-eye Tom Logan was born out of a yearning for the classic detectives of the1930s through the early 60s. Their golden era, when you might stumble upon a paperback with an image of a tough, hard-boiled gumshoe with a redhead on one arm and a smoking .45 at the end of the other. A cover illustrator's interpretation of the type of detective found within its pages. P.I.s like those created by authors Raymond Chandler, Dashiell Hammett, and later, Mickey Spillane, whose characters: Phillip Marlowe, Sam Spade, and Mike Hammer would soon become American icons of early detective fiction. The Tom Logan novels, starting with 'Anything Short of Murder,' through the latest, "Murder Is Such Sweet Revenge,' is an homage to those detectives and a throwback to a time when private-eyes used their wits instead of a computer, and muscle rather than a test-tube, to solve their cases.

Death Hides Behind a Mask
By
Tony Piazza

The envelope didn't need to have black around the edges to tell me that its contents foretold death. The address was written crudely, as if to disguise its sender, and there was no return. This attempt at deception confused me, however; for, after I carefully slit it open with the edge of my scissor and slid it out using the back of a pencil, the message inside wasn't cryptic at all. In fact, it was surprisingly frank. It read: 'If you want to stop the killings meet me in the old funhouse, Venice Beach Amusement Pier—midnight tonight. Come alone- no cops, or the girl dies', and it was signed 'Full Moon Killer.' I'll admit the signature was over the top, but I can't blame the writer. It was a brand placed upon him by the local press, who are never shy when it comes to sensationalism. Why should they be—the practice sells papers.

The rein of terror created by the appearance of this 'Full Moon Killer' began the earlier part of this year— January 14th to be exact, with the disappearance of a woman in her mid-twenties, who, on her way home alone from a late movie, apparently crossed the murderer's path. Her body was found a week later in the Silver Lake District, lying on a weedy hillside, fully dressed, and physically unmolested except for an eighth of an inch puncture wound at the base of her skull. About a month later on February 13th another victim was found, this time a male, age thirty, in an empty lot up in the Hollywood Hills. There was no sign of a struggle, but again the cause of death was from a sharp object, one-eighth of an inch in diameter entering at the back of the neck, just below the skull's base and driven up at an angle into the brain's medulla.

When a third victim—a middle-aged female, was discovered on March 14th on an isolated section of Venice Beach, it became apparent that the city was dealing with a serial killer. A murderer who appears to select his victims at random then kills them at some isolated spot, utilizing a thin, needle-like weapon thrust up into the brain. In all three of these cases there wasn't a sign of a struggle, or molestation in any form, and most interestingly had seemed to occur at specific intervals, when the moon was at its fullest phase; hence the epithet, "Full Moon Killer".

Why I should receive this summons was a mystery. It was a police case. Hendricks in Homicide was the point man for the LAPD. He was the guy most quoted in the papers. Who, depending on his mood, was either making threats to the killer or appeals to the public. If the murderer was to contact anyone it would be he, not me. I hadn't a clue why I was chosen. I was a speck on flypaper; a gumshoe who hadn't been around long enough to even make second billing.

I'd only set up shop in Hollywood recently. It took a portion of my savings and loans for the rest to get this private investigation business going. It was a rocky start. I was with the LAPD but tangled with a guy who had friends in high places. I made the mistake of having scruples as far as my job was concerned. I was even naïve to think that carrying a star meant that you played by the rules, kept your nose clean, and maintained the peace. Sadly, I was mistaken. It wasn't how things worked around here and I was too stubborn, idealistic, and morally conscientious to play it any other way.

Realizing that I couldn't be bribed or bullied, one of those powerful slime balls started shaking one of those gnarled trees in this Eden we call Los Angeles—a supposedly solid arbor referred to as a city politician, and a forbidden fruit came falling out; a nice, juicy, poison apple, better known as a frame-up. The scenario was fairly simple: send me out to bust a bootlegger, warn the bootlegger of my coming, and see what happens. There could only be two outcomes; one, I could end up dead, or two, I'd arrest him, in which case they'd arrange that he cry police brutality. During the raid, the guy attacks me, and so I'd had to get rough in self-defense- therefore the latter came into play. During the hearing, even my partner dummies up, and a plea bargain is made—either walk or jail time. Given little choice I handed in my resignation.

So, what's left for a man to do—no job and we're in a depression? Fortunately, going along with this arrangement as I did, they'd inadvertently left me an option. By them dropping the charges, I'd no record. Therefore, I was able to apply to get my own PI license and go into business for myself.

Presently, I was seated in that little cracker box I call an office. A space rented on the 5th floor, of an art deco office building at Hollywood Blvd and Gower. Just a simple room consisting of four walls, two windows—with limited view—and a functioning door that gives you access to this grand palace. Its furnishings were also as impressive: a desk, two chairs, and a gray metal filing cabinet—oh, and an office bottle and two glasses which I kept in the lower drawer of that desk in case I was planning to entertain royalty.

I was thinking about that bottle now as I tapped my fingers lightly against the blotter. No, I reasoned, better to keep a level head and determine my next move. There were no two ways about it; the LAPD would have to be notified about this letter. And even though its sender specified no police involvement, it had to be their call.

Grabbing my hat, I left the office and took the elevator to the ground floor. I was still a new enough tenant that a phone hadn't been connected in my office. Therefore any calls that had to be made were done so from a booth in the lobby.

After dropping in a nickel, I dialed the exchange and asked the switchboard operator for Homicide.

"Yeah, Inspector Hendricks, speaking; what can I do for you?"

"Hendricks," I repeated. "This is Tom Logan. I just received something that may interest you."

"Hey, Logan, how the hell are you?"

"Fine," I answered shortly, anxious to get to the point. "I think I've gotten a letter from the 'Full Moon Killer'."

"Good for you," he responded with a yawn. "We got a half dozen as well."

"So what do you want me to do with it?"

"File it."

"You kidding?"

"Naw." He then explained: "Killings like this bring out all kinds of loonies—mostly lonely guys who are looking for attention. They think taking credit for a spectacular crime will give them some notoriety. Why anyone would want that kind of fame is beyond me."

"I think you may want to read this one," I stated firmly.

"Why, is it written in blood?"

"It mentions a female hostage, and a time, and place. It also says no police, and asks that I come alone."

"Oh, yeah," he responded growing suddenly suspicious, "Why you? Maybe you're the guy that's needing the attention?"

"Don't be ridiculous, Hendricks, I'm not that desperate for business - and in answer to your question, I've been asking it myself."

"Well, nevertheless," he continued, "tonight I can't take the risk of putting all my eggs into one basket. It's April 13th—a full moon, in case you don't know—and what little manpower I have will have to be spread across the entire county because no one knows exactly where this bastard's going to strike next."

"That's just it," I argued. "*There is a full moon tonight* and this letter's telling us plainly where and when he plans to strike."

"As did all my other letters and, following them up, we came up blank."

Realizing our discussion was going nowhere I finally asked what he wanted me to do.

"Do whatever the hell you want, Logan," was his response. I told him in all conscience I had to make the appointment. At this, he somewhat relented. "Look, he mentioned the pier at Venice Beach, right?"

"Yes; the old funhouse at the Amusement Pier—midnight."

"I thought they tore that down after the fire?"

"So did I, but apparently not."

"Well, I still think this is a wild goose chase, but if you insist on going, I'll see if I can spare a car to patrol the area."

"Thanks," I answered sourly, and hung up.

The rest of the morning and afternoon moved at a crawl. There were no new clients or problems to occupy my time. That was the trouble with this business: it's either feast or famine—and most times my plate was empty, which doesn't pay the bills. Around 4:35 I removed the .45 from my holster, slipped out its clip, and after verifying that there wasn't a bullet in the chamber, carefully cleaned and oiled its moveable parts. I've learned from time spent in the army, as well as four years on the force, that a gun is like a surgeon's scalpel, if you show it care and keep it rust free, it just may save a life. Of course, they were thinking of its bearer. With regards to the person facing its business end, that may be an entirely different story.

I locked up around six and had a bite at the food counter in The Owl Drug store located in the Professional Building on Hollywood Boulevard at Sycamore Avenue. Nothing fancy, just a sandwich and black coffee. After that I wasted half an hour at Whitey's Newsstand and then about an hour at the Satyr bookstore at Vine. Sometime around 8:30 pm I caught a Red Car to begin my journey to Venice Beach.

I hadn't gotten around to getting an automobile yet. In fact, on my budget, I couldn't afford one anytime soon. It's certainly a disadvantage in my business, especially if there are instances when you need to get across town in a hurry. When called for I've borrowed a friend's automobile; but only when it was absolutely necessary and never without fair warning. In this instance, however, I hadn't much notice, and so it was public transportation—a street car—that eventually took me to what might turn out to be my rendezvous with death.

The beach town of Venice is located 14 miles west of Los Angeles. Founded in 1905 by Abbott Kinney, a tobacco millionaire and his business partner Francis Ryan, the resort was originally called "Venice of America". Canals in its residential district, crossed by arched bridges and navigated by gondola tour boats, played to this image of its Italian namesake, as did the block-long businesses which reflected Venetian architecture. The biggest draw, however, was the mile long beach, rental cottages, and amusement pier, complete with three roller coasters, game booths, a tall Dragon Slide, and many other attractions.

It was slightly after nine when I stepped from the Red Car. The sun had long since sunk into the ocean, and the pier and its surrounding businesses were shut up for the night. I'd stumbled upon the occasional passerby as I'd wandered the area but, being that it was a week night, and the air unusually chilly, the crowd one normally gets during the height of the season was markedly absent. I still had a little less than three hours before my appointment and so directed my steps to the business district, and a small speakeasy I knew quietly resided there.

I allowed myself a couple glasses of Scotch for fortitude and nursed them in a corner, listening to a Negro combo playing New Orleans style jazz. This ate up another hour and a half so, by 11:00, I was once again loitering across from the pier's entrance.

Evidently, Hendricks wasn't living up to his promise. For all that time I'd spent walking the streets I didn't see one patrol car pass by, and as I stood in the shadow of a shuttered shell shop, gazing at the single circle of light cast from a street lamp across the road, I was feeling very much alone.

Drawing up my shoulders I pressed ahead, deciding that it was either now or never. Fog had settled in, drifting in on a light breeze from the Pacific. A shiver suddenly crept up my spine, but I doubted very much that it was caused by the weather. A dark hole yawned in front of me—the wide walkway between the amusement arcades. And even though a full moon was floating somewhere above me, the low clouds were preventing its light from illuminating my way.

A small hut was off to the side, just as you passed under the broad arch of the entrance, announcing, 'The Venice Pier'. A dull light could be seen in its lone window, emanating from the office of the night watchman. I decided it was probably a good idea to check in with him; let him know that I'd be wandering the premises and why, and instruct him, for his own safety, to steer clear of the old funhouse. As it turned out, it wasn't necessary. Through the window I could see that the old man seated inside was fast asleep - passed out by the look of it. There was an empty bottle near his elbow, and, as I eased open the door, the air inside reeked of cheap liquor. I didn't bother to wake him, deciding it would be a waste of time. He'd probably be out for hours.

I looked at the illuminated dials on my wrist watch. It was now ten after eleven. There were still 50 minutes left until the appointment. It's funny how time seems to crawl when you're keeping track of it. After gingerly easing the door shut again, I proceeded at a casual pace down the length of the midway. Uneasiness accompanied me as I passed from one closed up booth to another and from their shadows I imagined probing eyes upon me. Fortunately, there was the comforting feel of a holster lying snugly under my left armpit. Automatically, I reached down and loosened the button of my jacket, letting it fall open so I could easily reach the .45 tucked neatly inside.

Eventually the walkway between the buildings widened to a large open space where the carnival rides began. I unconsciously made a mental note of their fanciful names as I passed each of their entrances: 'Racing Derby', 'Noah's Ark', 'Mill Chutes', and 'Flying Circus', to mention only a few. There were also the traditional Ferris wheel and Merry-Go-Round which, normally ablaze with colorful lights and gay music, now stood eerily dark and mute in the misty night. In the distance to both sides and dead ahead of me, I saw the outlines of the three roller coasters, their gray, weather-worn wooden superstructures resembling the bones of some long dead leviathans whose mates were still mourning their passing from a distance, with a cry that strongly resembled a foghorn.

I reached what I took was the center of the park and an intersection that went off at 90° in all four directions. It had been awhile since I'd visited this pier but, if my memory served me right, the old funhouse was located in the west end.

Around a year ago there had been a fire and a portion of the pier's western section was damaged. Three of the attractions, including the building housing the funhouse were casualties of the blaze and closed ever since. A new funhouse was eventually erected but at the opposite side of the park because the pilings at this western section were deemed unstable and scheduled for removal.

Cost, however, had delayed demolition and so, as I neared the charred pier, I spied gates barring the way, posted with warnings of **'DANGER'**, and **'NO PERSONS BEYOND THIS POINT.'** Again I looked at my watch; it was a quarter until midnight. There was a sturdy looking railing nearby and I leaned against it, presumably to stall for time, but actually using the minutes constructively for one last, careful examination of the surroundings.

Several yards beyond the barrier stood the old funhouse, a two-story, white clapboard building which, at a first glance, seemed untouched by the disaster but actually showed evidence of smoke damage and partial roof collapse. A ticket booth sat in the middle, and an entrance way and exit situated alongside either end. There were painted cutouts of clowns, and of seals balancing balls on the tips of their noses—there was even a rotund couple frozen in a fit of laughter—all decorating its exterior but most were either faded, water stained, or partly obscured by thick layers of soot.

Five until midnight.

Fishing out a flashlight—which I'd the sense to bring along—I switched on the beam being careful to direct it low.

I needed to see where I was going, but preferred to do so without advertising my approach.

The barriers turned out to be no problem, just waist high portable gates that any five year old could move with his little finger. Why someone even bothered was a mystery to me. Easily I skirted between them and then warily cut across the no-man's land up ahead. At this stage my heart had crept into my throat. If someone was planning an ambush it would be here, where I was most vulnerable. Fortunately, that wasn't the case and, with a sense of relief, made it to the entrance without incident.

I climbed some rickety stairs—purposely designed that way for the attraction and not as a result of the fire—and attaining the second floor, crossed a short suspension bridge that led to a balcony. The slats on the bridge were solid and supported by heavy chains so, even though they creaked and groaned with my every step, I'd confidence that they'd hold.

The door I entered off the balcony led into a hall of mirrors or, perhaps more accurately, a maze of them. As I first stepped into the room I was startled by my own reflection and, embarrassed to say, drew my .45 and pointed at it. Luckily, I recognized what it was before pulling the trigger. More warily after that, I continued on, weaving along the path of the maze, making sure that I didn't get too trigger happy in the process.

As I reached the end I suddenly started getting this feeling again of being watched. Only this time, it was stronger and seemed more malevolent in intent. I would've chalked it up to imagination, except, soon after, the breathing started.

"Who's there?" I cried out.

The sound was close and asthmatic.

"I have a gun," I warned.

There was still no response.

Up ahead, through a doorway, I could see a faint light. With caution, I advanced toward it, my senses keenly probing for any signs of danger as I stepped softly in its direction. When I'd reached the threshold I paused and examined its interior. The room was filled with cut-outs of barrels - large ones, small ones, some piled atop another, and others tilted like they were about to fall. In the center of the enclosure was a giant one, on its side and open at both ends. In its heyday it would spin as guests tried to navigate through it with sometimes hilarious results. What I now saw lying in its static interior, however, was anything but amusing. A redhead, perhaps in her twenties, stripped to her silky, cream colored slip, and tied hand and foot stretched upon the floor. At first I wasn't sure if she was still alive but, after watching her for some moments, she began to squirm and I could see some heaving of her ample breasts.

"You Ok?" I asked in a whisper. I know it was a dumb question but, under the circumstances, it seemed appropriate.

This got her trying to rise and look in my direction. She got as far as lifting herself onto one elbow and turning her head so her eyes met mine. She was an attractive girl, nice figure, flawless skin, and pretty face. Presently she was gagged - a dirty cloth across her mouth and tied behind her head. She tried saying something but the words were muffled and unrecognizable. Her gaze, however, spoke volumes. It was full of fright and desperation. There was also a glassiness about them, as if just waking from a drugged sleep.

"You men are predictable." The voice startled me, coming suddenly from the back of the room and piercing the silence. It was thin, high pitched, and bitter. She continued, "See an attractive, half naked girl and they'll let their guard down every time." Her words struck me like the sting of a poisonous, spitting viper, and before I could see who'd uttered it, two enormous arms encircled me from behind, pinning both my arms to my sides.

"See what I mean?" the earlier voice mocked and it was followed by a laugh that told me the owner wasn't dealing from a fully stacked deck.

I tried struggling loose, but without luck. The goon just applied more pressure and my arms began to feel numb.

"It's nice to see you again, Logan."

I still couldn't see who was speaking so I answered into thin air. "Do we know each other?"

"Oh, indeed we do," the female voice returned with emphasis.

At this point she stepped out from behind one of the cutouts: a petite woman, dressed in a rather drab gray skirt, and dirty white blouse. However, as to who she was – well, that still remained a mystery. An elastic mask, the type hospitals use to cover severe burn victims to protect them from infection, was concealing her face. All I could see was what was revealed in its openings—two shining eyes, a thin nose, and a slit for a mouth.

"I'm afraid, I still don't—" I began, but she interrupted with a sharp command.

"Drop the gun."

It wasn't doing much good where I presently had it directed thanks to the gorilla behind me - pointed at the floor; but still, I wasn't about to relinquish it so easily.

"I've an inferiority complex," I answered. "I'd rather hold onto it, if you don't mind."

"But I do." She nodded at the guy behind me. I couldn't see his features either, but definitely felt his strength. I could also tell that he had me beat when it came to height and weight. He applied some more pressure, and I thought I felt a rib crack. Still I held stubbornly onto my weapon.

"Ok," she responded, decisively. "Let's try something else." She walked over to the girl, and kneeling by her side produced a thin ice pick which she raised threateningly, as if to strike at a point at the back of her neck. "Care to have her blood on your hands?"

The girl started to squirm more frantically, as desperation filled her eyes.

"What's it, Logan?" she chided impatiently, "The gun or the girl?"

I swallowed hard and dropped the weapon.

"Good boy." She nodded again at the guy behind me, and I felt him ease his grip. But before I got full use of my arms I felt something strike hard at the back of my skull, and I was out for the count.

When I drifted out of the blackness I found myself on the floor next to the redhead and trussed up pretty much as she, minus the gag. The woman was staring down at me, as was her trained monkey, and I was right about him. He was tall, well over 6'5" and at least 265 pounds of hardened muscle. He could've been a wrestler or boxer. He seemed dim-witted enough. His two dark brown eyes were expressionless, wide spaced, and seated on either side of a flattened, crooked nose, obviously broken at some time. Two ears - one cauliflower, stood out from a mass of thick, blue-black hair. The skin on his face was scarred and pitted and sagged alongside a mouth that was wide and down-turned. It gave him the appearance of a bulldog.

"This is Carlos, Logan," introduced the woman, who'd obviously noted my careful examination of the man. "He's been my right hand."

"Ok," I answered, finding my voice. "Now I know who the organ grinder's pet is, but I still can't place your face—or what little I can see of it."

"Very well," she responded, as if making up her mind. "But there's still no guarantee you'll recognize it."

With that she pulled off the mask and the face that appeared sneering down at me was shocking. It was a death head defined. Shrunken, shallow cheeks, high cheek bones, and deeply set eyes, with flesh the texture of a walnut. Raw in spots, red and blistery with patches of white. The closest thing I could think to describe it would be the marbling of uncooked meat.

"Pretty isn't it," she sneered through her teeth which were broken and stained yellow. A side of her lip was also puffy, drawing its corner down into a permanent, lopsided grimace. "I didn't always look like this." She reached up and brushed back a few hairs that were plastered against her damp forehead. They were thin, and colorless like the rest of her. It was cut boyishly short, and when she tried to fluff it up, it stood at odd angles in the spots that weren't balding.

Slowly, she took a step forward and then crouched down so we were now at eye level, drawing up so close in fact that I could smell her rancid breath.

"Still no clue, Logan?"

I shook my head, but an idea was starting to take shape. A distant memory—well, perhaps not so distant—a recollection which I'd worked hard to forget in the time that'd gone by. Still, I waited, wanting her to tell me.

"Alice," she offered, with hateful eyes, searching for signs of recognition within my own. "Alice Munson." She must've caught my blink at the divulging of her name because she continued more confidently, "You were responsible for this, Logan..." She pointed toward her face. "...you and all the others that set me up."

In a sense there was a kernel of truth in that, but only just. Undoubtedly all that she'd gone through has confused the facts in her mind.

I'd met Alice Munson three years ago, while fresh on the force. I'd encouraged her to testify against a small-time mobster who was running a protection racket on my beat.

She was a pretty girl then—much like the woman tied up beside me. I think she'd won some sort of beauty contest back east, at some small town in Pennsylvania, if I'm not mistaken. There was a so-called talent agent in the audience who'd convinced her and her family that she was a prime candidate for moving pictures. It's the same old story; the guy either wanted a good time, good money or both. He got the whole enchilada with Alice, and when he was through with her, he dumped what was left in the middle of Hollywood Boulevard. With no money, prospects, and ashamed to write home, she made out the best she could with what little she had—namely, her looks.

She started picking up tricks on her own, but then a John got wise and gave her options—move on, or cut him in. Not accepting either would mean suffering dire consequences, so she went to work for him.

Her biggest hangout was a speakeasy on Sunset and that's where she met Leo Delgetti—a small time hood with big ideas. He took a shine to Alice and offered her the world if she'd leave the streets and become his own personal trophy. Of course, she agreed and he in turn granted her wish to make it in pictures. As I said, he was small potatoes when it came to some of the other east coast boys, but he did have some influence in the picture business—mainly small-fry, like assistant directors and casting agents. Eventually he got her some background work and a few bit parts.

All seemed to be going well, but then she started to get the big head and, after a minor affair with an actor, decided she didn't need Delgetti any longer. He made it hell for her after that, and she realized she'd never be free of him unless he was dead or locked up in jail. She didn't have a stomach for the former, but the latter seemed a reasonable possibility.

An investigation was going on at the time—Vice was looking into protection rackets in the city. Don't ask me why Alice chose me. I was just a cop on the beat. Maybe it was because I'd happened to patrol the neighborhood that housed her apartment. In any case she approached me with an offer to testify against Delgetti in exchange for protection. I told her to go to Vice but she told me she was afraid to and asked that I arrange it for her.

To make a long story short, I did, but the boys in Vice botched it. Maybe there was someone on Delgetti's payroll in the department, or even the DA's office, but after a short and very one-sided hearing the guy got off, and Alice was made to pay for her betrayal.

It was less than a week after the conclusion of the investigation. The boys still had her hid away in a cheap hotel on East 3rd, but someone must have snitched. Her protection for that evening suddenly disappeared, and a man broke through the door, pinning her to the floor and throwing vitriol into her face. He got away, and not surprisingly, no one bothered to tie Delgetti in with the assault.

Alice survived—but not her mind, as she was bounced from one hospital to another, until she eventually was committed as a permanent fixture in the psychiatric ward of the Santa Fe Railroad Hospital in Boyle Heights.

"So, they let you out?" I asked, trying to sound conversational and casual while, behind my back, I was groping for something sharp to free my bonds.

"No, Carlos helped me escape." She turned her head slightly in the giant's direction and I saw softness creep momentarily into her eyes. "We've become good friends, he and I. Haven't we Carlos?"

The man grunted.

"Carlos is a deaf mute," she explained shortly, "and as docile as a kitten."

"Except when he does your bidding," I added.

A portion of the inside of the rotating barrel was constructed of sheet metal. I located a rough seam where two panels were joined. Fortunately, it was conveniently located low, and within easy reach. If careful, I could work at the rope, keeping my actions hidden behind my back. And the best way to do that, I'd decided, was to keep her talking.

"Carlos loves me," she shouted. "He doesn't care about outward appearances, only what's inside."

"Sure… sure," I returned appeasingly. "Beauty is only skin deep."

"You're saying that because you figure it's what I want to hear," she barked back. Her aggressiveness a barometer telling me that I was dealing with an imbalanced state of mind. I decided to try another approach.

"If you're seeking revenge, and I assume that's what this is all about, why take the trouble to make it look like the work of a serial killer?"

"It's payback, alright. And if you cops weren't so dumb you could've figured it out." She held out her hand and started counting them off on each of her skeletal-like fingers. "Victim one, Ann Compton—one of Delgetti's girls —refused to back up my witness against him; victim two, Robert Curry—Delgetti's bookkeeper—promised to provide evidence but later said he was mistaken and finally, victim three, Linda Malone, Delgetti's ex-girlfriend, who lied to protect him, under oath at the hearing."

"And, I take it you're blaming me for setting you up with Vice."

"No," she shouted, "for handing me over to a crooked cop in that department—the bastard who sold me out. I expected better from you."

"I'd no way of knowing," I argued, "And besides, why not go after him?"

Obviously I wasn't suggesting that, but needed to keep the conversation going to distract her from the actions going on behind my back. I was a quarter of the way through the rope.

"I plan to," she answered shortly. "And there's a few more on my hit list."

"Including Delgetti?"

"Especially Delgetti, but he won't be easy - too much protection."

She was starting to act distracted, as evidenced by her shorter answers. The last thing I wanted was for her to start thinking about that ice pick. I needed to buy more time.

"You haven't answered my question about this ruse of yours—this 'Full Moon Killer' routine."

"It wasn't my idea. You can thank the press for that."

"But, the killings," I queried. "...And only during the full moon?"

"At first it was simply a matter of convenience. I needed light for my work. You have to understand, we were on the run from those seeking me from the asylum, hiding by day and moving after dark. Scrounging for food and drink. My victims provided some cash, but mostly Carlos stealing what he could from waste bins and grocery stores along the way. For obvious reasons, I couldn't be seen in the light, so we found places to hide by day. Carlos abducted those I pointed out to him and brought them to a remote area at night so I could inflict my punishments upon them. A full moon served my purpose—before their deaths I could show my face and reveal the real reason for their executions."

There was a glazed, far-away look in her eyes as she told her story. After awhile, I'd realized she was no longer talking to me, but re-living the moments for herself. That suited me fine; while she rambled on I was working feverishly on my bonds and making good progress.

"After the first two jobs," she continued, "I became aware of the press calling this a serial killing and labelling me the 'Full Moon Killer.' So, why not use it, and I did," she concluded and cognizance came leaping back into her gaze.

I'd sawed through half the cord, but that wasn't enough to force it apart. I needed a few seconds more.

"What about this place?" I asked.

She looked about, as if seeing it for the first time, and then answered, "We discovered this in our travels about a week ago. It's not the Ritz, but it gives us a roof over our heads—and privacy—condemned as it is..." She then turned viciously toward my fellow captive and lashed out, "until this BITCH stumbled onto Carlos the other night—something had to be done—so he grabbed her—and, as it turns out, she's proved useful—as a lure for the trap I've set for you."

She was working up to the grand finale. I could tell by the way she was now rushing her explanations—as if to say, "Let's get on with it." I needed a moment more.

"They'll catch you, you know. The police may be slow in making the connection but you'll screw up—actually, from what you've told me, you've already been taking a lot of risks. Honestly, I think you've been extremely lucky so far."

"Well, before they do, I'm taking as many with me as I can. Do you think I want to keep living like this? I'd welcome death."

"But what if they take you alive—"

"Enough!" she shouted. Obviously, I'd pushed it as far as I could. "Let's conclude this. It'll be quick, and both your bodies—splash—into the Pacific. We don't even have to go far." She indicated over her shoulder. "There's a hole back there in the planking."

I looked over at Carlos who'd been watching her quietly the entire time, like a dog waiting for instructions from his mistress. After she'd finished this last speech she made some type of signal toward him. It didn't make any sense to me but obviously he understood because instantly he disappeared out of sight, only to return a moment later with a lantern. An old fashion kerosene lamp, whose wick was giving off a warm, yellow glow.

"Now," she continued, fingering the ice pick. "Who wants to go first?"

As she said this, I once again applied force at my wrists and was finally able to snap my bonds. Simultaneously, the ape had been advancing with the lamp while leaning forward to provide more light for his mistress. I used that moment to brace myself with my newly freed arms and kick with all my force in the direction of the lamp. It connected, knocking it from his hands and causing it to shatter near the crazed woman. A trail of kerosene, with its traveling flame, splattered across the floor boards, catching fire to the hem of her skirt and immediately spreading upwards to engulf her. Frantically I pulled loose the rope around my ankles and then started for her, intending to tackle her to the ground and assist her by rolling her back and forth on the floor to extinguish the flames.

Carlos unfortunately misread my intentions and rushed for my gun where it still lay on the floor. The woman was screaming like a banshee and doing exactly what she shouldn't. Rushing out of the barrel, she was running aimlessly around the room further feeding the flames.

"Let me help her, dammit," I shouted as I watched the . 45 swing in my direction. It was wasted breath; the ape couldn't understand. Helplessly, I could see his finger tighten on the trigger as, at the same instant, I could hear the frightened, muffled gasps from the redhead behind. I figured we were done for. And when the shot came, I was waiting for the impact of the bullet; but, surprisingly, it never came. I was stunned because I knew at that close range he couldn't have missed, and surprised when the answer soon became apparent.

At first, the ape had gotten this surprised look on his face and then he started to turn away. However, the pain was too much and part way he dropped onto his knees, revealing as he fell, a man behind him, standing with legs apart in the doorway. It was Hendricks, a thin trail of blue smoke rising from the muzzle of his police revolver.

"Logan," he shouted, "you, Ok?"

"Yeah," I cried back, "Nice of you to stop by."

"You're welcome, too," he returned. "But, I suggest we hightail it out of here, pronto. This place is a tinder box."

I didn't bother to answer but, lifting the redhead into my arms, ran for the door. Out of the corner of my eye I could see the room was already enveloped in flames and somewhere within this inferno, undoubtedly, lay the charred body of Alice Munson, who finally got her wish.

* * *

"Feeling any better now?" I asked the redhead, whose name I found out was Katie. She worked at the pier and, forgetting her purse the other night, returned after closing to retrieve it. That was when she unfortunately stumbled onto Carlos. At the present, she was bundled up in a blanket provided by the fire department, who was fighting a losing battle with the flames. Last I heard they were going to let the building burn, and just make sure that the blaze didn't spread to the rest of the pier. The boys in blue were also present, but under the circumstances there was little they could do.

The girl smiled weakly at my question, showing dimples and a row of even white teeth. "I guess so," she answered slowly. "Thanks for coming to my rescue."

"Don't thank me," I responded, honestly. "I darned near mucked it up. If you want to thank anyone it would be the inspector."

Hendricks was standing close by and overheard me.

"Let's say we both had a hand in this," he commented over his shoulder. "You led us to the killer."

"I appreciate that," I responded. "But you could've told me you were providing backup."

"It was a last minute decision. I almost decided against it."

"I'm glad you had second thoughts."

He ignored my sorry wit, and continued, "When I did decide to follow, I thought it best to keep a low profile until you'd made contact. I and my men were pretty much on your tail since you arrived here earlier this evening."

That explained that feeling of being watched as I made my way down the midway.

"What surprised me," the redhead interjected, "was the intensity of hatred that woman showed. In one respect I can understand it, but in another I couldn't believe it of my gender."

I quoted: "I think Nietzsche said it best: 'In revenge and in love woman is more barbaric than man.'"

"I think I'd prefer the love part," she answered seriously.

Gazing down at the lovely features of her face as a hint of suggestion suddenly appeared in her shinning green eyes, I couldn't help but say to myself that I'd have to agree.

Mary Moses

I've been writing for many years in one format or another--6 years at *The Sun* newspaper and 14 years of newsletters for all the educational employees in the county. Then I got serious. I have nine books published, both fiction and non-fiction. I lived in San Luis Obispo County for decades, and moved to Sonoma County six years ago to be nearer to my son--who promptly got a job in New Jersey.

Lately I've concentrated on my art work, until I came across an assignment for the Sisters (in May 2006) when Sue challenged the members at a SinC meeting to write the minutes of that meeting in the style of a famous detective. So I assumed the persona of A.C. Doil and wrote of his two famous characters: Homes and his assistant, Watts. It was only a small leap to "Minutes of the Meeting." I'm feeling the twinges of creativity again.Time to return to writing on a regular basis.

Minutes of the Meeting

by

Mary Moses

The meeting of the Tuesday Tea and Culture Club was called to order by the President, Mrs. James "Zizi" Jellicoe. Before she could ask for the invocation and the introduction of guests, Mrs. Hedley "Polly" Hrodny rose from her chair, and without asking for the floor, took a pistol from her purse and shot the President dead.

The quick-thinking Vice-President, Miss Belinda Barrows, immediately assumed the Chairmanship and called for order in the house. She asked the Parliamentarian for the proper procedure for notifying the police. This had been done ad hoc.

Belinda, now President Pro-Tem, asked that luncheon be delayed for a half-hour. The members concurred unanimously.

Polly Hrodny calmly sat down and slowly placed her pistol on the table, next to the salad fork. She sat upright, looking forward, saying nothing.

Two policemen arrived in short order; they were Sergeant Chaz Copley, Jr., and his assistant William Walker III. The Sergeant took charge immediately, without so much as asking for permission to speak.

"What's goin' on here?" he said.

The Parliamentarian gave him the pertinent details, whereupon he turned to Polly and asked, "Why'd ya do it, lady?"

As she answered, he slowly, and with great care, lifted the gun from the table and handed it to his assistant.

"My husband was messing around with another woman—her." She pointed at Zizi.

"Yeah? How do you know?" Polly had his full attention.

"They spent last Saturday night at a motel. He had told me he would be out of town on business, but I knew he had lied to me. I had suspected that something was going on for quite a while. And when I drove by that place—late at night —there was his car. At that point, I knew what I had to do."

"So why not go after *him*?" The sergeant's eyebrows were in their upright and locked position.

"Oh, I took care of him this morning. I put ground glass in his granola."

"Well, I gotta take you in." He motioned for his assistant to open the door, and then, rather roughly, took Polly by the arm. As they walked across the room, the members quickly moved from their path.

All except Miss Raquel Romero, who approached the pair with an unusual smile on her face.

"So you go it all figured out?" she said to Polly, still smirking. "You've had it in for poor Zizi ever since she came to town last year. What a sap. You got the wrong woman. He was there with *me*. I'm the one he really loves, you clod."

A gasp went through the membership and a few cries of shock were heard. From the back of the room came a voice, "That jerk! He's been sweet-talking me for months. Told me I was his soul-mate and the only one he's ever truly loved."

"He made advances to me," another voice added, "but I had a cold that night. Good thing for me."

One member was heard to say that ground glass was too good for him.

The President Pro-Tem, now very pale, called again for order; her request was ignored.

"What about poor Zizi?" the Parliamentarian asked the Sergeant. "We can't just leave her there."

"I'll send someone over to take care of her," he said. In surveying the room, he said as he took Polly away, "Well, ladies, he strayed, but at least he stayed with members of the club."

The minutes of the previous meeting were read and approved.

There being no further business, the meeting was adjourned.

Respectfully submitted,
Mrs. Elva R. (Jane) Denison
Secretary

Janice Konstantinidis

Janice Konstantinidis was born in Australia. She migrated to the U.S.A. in 2005. She lives on the Central Coast of California with her husband and two dogs.

Janice spent the majority of her working life in the area of gerontology. She has a particular interest in delirium and dementia. Janice developed and managed a special care facility for people who were suffering from alcohol-related brain damage. This development of this facility took her almost ten years, and she looks back on it with a large amount of satisfaction.

Janice has always written in some form. She loves to write poetry and short stories. She is currently writing her memoir and a book of limericks.

The motivation to write 'Mistress Mine,' came from Janice's involvement with the writer's organisations, NightWriter's and Sisters in Crime. She'd noticed a call for submissions for an upcoming anthology from Sisters in Crime. Stories were called for from writers about murders on the central coast.

Going from poetry and memoir to murder, seemed like it would be quite a leap. The idea went out of her mind until she read an article about a dating site for married people. The thought of this didn't sit well with her, and it occurred to Janice that she may well have it in her to murder someone... just for the anthology, mind you.

Delinquent Diana was born. Janice enjoyed creating this character, with her righteous indignation. She can't see any reason why Diana should remain idle now.

Her vigilante character will strike again.

Mistress Mine
by
Janice Konstantinidis

Anita closed the motel door and began to walk. Breathing deeply, she inhaled the warm night air: taking in the delicious sense of freedom she felt surging through her veins. Killing Daniel had been easy.

He'd been watching TV with his back to her when she'd knocked him unconscious with a blow to the back of his head with a wrench. After injecting him with insulin to induce a coma, she dragged him to the bath. It had been a challenge, but she'd managed it. All had gone according to plan. Daniel was now soaking in potassium hydroxide with a bag of lime thrown in for good measure. Her husband had often stated his preference for chemical cremation.

Anita hoped he wouldn't be found for many hours. She'd left the 'Do Not Disturb' sign on the door. If all went as planned, he would be unrecognizable by the next evening. Anita had lain awake for weeks planning her methods, materials, route, alibi and cleanup.

When housekeeping staff discovered Daniel, he would be brown sludge. He'd never be identified. Anita knew Daniel had checked into the motel under a false name, and had paid cash to do so for three days. She had inside information, if you will. He'd be a John Doe in the San Luis Obispo County Morgue. Well, a John Doe Sludge....

Anita reached her car feeling exhilarated. She dropped her long dark wig in a dumpster and her party dress and pumps in a Goodwill drop off on the way home. Fresh jeans and a top felt good; her naturally red and short pixie cut felt snug around her head.

The new widow took a long drink from her orange juice and started her car. She had a quick drive to her home in San Luis Obispo. A shower and sleep would be wonderful. She had a tennis game mid-morning.

As she drove through the night, she felt more confident and much happier than she had in a long time. She would stay in San Luis Obispo for a week as planned and then head back to work in Santa Barbara. She was the executive director of their in-home nursing business; her input would be needed.

Daniel had been planning a trip back to Israel to see his elderly mother who hadn't been well. His friends in Santa Barbara were concerned; there was unrest in Tel Aviv, but Daniel was a stubborn man—every one knew it. When Anita announced next week that Daniel had left on a flight for Tel Aviv, no one would raise an eyebrow. He'd done this several times in the past. They had friends who owned private jets. Anita would express concern that she hadn't heard from Daniel. It would be a mystery.

Friends would ultimately assume that Syrian rebels had taken Daniel. Not such an uncommon thing when one was as politically vocal as Daniel. It would be seen as a tragic ending. Poor Anita.

Daniel and Anita's marriage had been more companionate than romantic for some time. Anita believed that Daniel, at 55, had reached 'that' age where men had erectile dysfunction, or so he'd said. His interest in her had waned. She had missed the intimacy initially; however, her losses were assuaged by a multi-million dollar home in San Luis Obispo, a BMW, the condominium in Palm Springs and, of course, their showcase home in Santa Barbara. Good friends and a close community provided a surfeit of company, which softened the emptiness of the marital bed. They had no children. Their in-home care giving business was showing an excellent profit, with over one eighty on-call employees, and she had to say that life was very good until one day, about two months ago.

Anita had been looking in Daniel 's office for business information. When she turned on his computer, she saw email from a dating site that said he had "New Matches." This set off an alarm in Anita's mind. She began searching his desk. She wanted to log into the dating site. She found his user name and password in a memo book in a corner of a drawer.

Anita was horrified at what she found on the site. She saw that he had been logged in less than three hours previously. She read Daniel 's profile . . .

" I am what you could call an innovator of lust. A purveyor of pleasure... an oracle of orgasm. My interests vary; while I enjoy conventional vanilla sex, my true self comes to the fore, as it were, when I can be a master to a naughty, bad, subservient woman. I like all forms of eroticism, pain, and bondage. I am a maestro of all things sexual and will conduct my ballet of rhapsody with a baton of steel... Erectile Eric."

Anita's heart was racing. She felt sick, and could read no more. Daniel? Her Daniel! Thoughts ricocheted from one side of her mind to the other. This had to be some kind of joke...no matter how unfaithful he'd been, he was not the man she'd read about in that profile. It was all fantasy, or so she thought. She'd known Daniel since they were in high school, and she would have known if he had any of these tendencies. This had to be a mid-age crisis. Yes, that was what this was. She opened a bottle of water from Daniels' bar fridge in his office.

She read several messages that her husband had sent and received from numerous women, one in particular, which were dated some months ago. Anita left the office for the day angered by what she had read.

It was clear that Daniel had been involved with several women over the months, and it was probable that more had been going on. She had begun to read about a side of Daniel she couldn't identify, much less believe. She had to know more.

Later that evening Anita logged into Hotmail and created an account for herself. She then created an account on the dating site, writing up a very feisty profile. The site's logo read: "Life is short. Have an affair."

"I am an attached and wanton wench, in need of some fine loving. I am open to new things. I love to cuddle. I suspect I am a quite a naughty girl at heart, I just need that right 'touch.' Yours lustfully, Delinquent Dianna."

A waiting game had begun... a short waiting game, as it turned out. When Anita checked back after dinner, she found an email from Erectile Eric in 'Delinquent Diana's' inbox.

"Well hello, Delinquent Diana! How nice to see your lovely face. Would you care to write more, you certainly have my attention?' Anita's bait had been taken... Daniel had found her profile.

The photo she'd posted was of her friend in New York City—a woman Daniel hadn't met, and a good looker. Anita wrote back: " Dear Erectile Eric, I am a very bad girl who needs to be taught how to tow the line, to be spanked until am very contrite. I was beyond excitement when I read your profile, sending you a wink, Yours, Delinquent Dianna." Anita had become Delinquent Diana in a millisecond.

Anita noted that Daniel seemed very upbeat the next day on their daily walk at lunchtime; even the office manager Rosa noticed it, commenting, "San Luis Obispo agrees with you Daniel, you should try to go there every weekend. You know what they say about too much work and no play." Anita noticed that Daniel looked in the other direction.

Anita squirmed. She had to hand it to him, he was eager; there was an email waiting for Delinquent Diana when Anita logged into her new email account, along with a couple of other notifications from "Lushly Addison," as well as other men. Anita was surprised by the intensity of her feelings. She was very angry at her husband's attraction to this fantasy female.

Delinquent Diana was attracting lots of attention. Eight men had contacted her. Looking at the men's profiles, Anita noticed that they were all married. *What is going on?* she thought as she quickly changed her status to married. *"This was, after all, a dating site for married people"*, she mused. Daniel had checked the married box as well. *What is with all this? It's so wrong,* she thought, and felt a surge of indignation and anger. *A dating site for people who are married? Incredible,* thought Anita.

Eric's reply to Delinquent Diana was catchy and charming. He'd invited her to use his email address so they wouldn't need to go through the dating site. Delinquent Diana sent him a quick reply with her email address.

Anita was going to have to calm down if she was to get to the bottom of this. She was very angry; Daniel had not been this sweet to *her* in years.

She decided to write to another man, as research, and soon found a likely candidate in Robert. He was also a man who wanted to control women. His profile mentioned a need to be a father to naughty girl. Anita sighed, and sent him Delinquent Diana's profile. He was quick to respond and offered the option of writing to his email address. There seemed to be a need with these men to establish closer contact quite quickly. She would later learn that men paid to contact women on the site, and they liked to use a minimum amount of 'credits'.

Anita's curiosity had been piqued by the various profiles she'd read. It was another world to her... Robert wrote that he was highly successful in his work, married for twenty years, no longer sexually active in his marriage but not prepared to leave his wife. He told Delinquent Diana that he was in the computer programming business and had become very adept at having affairs, and that his work took him all over the country and sometimes overseas. He asked Delinquent Diana for a phone number. She told him she'd think about it. Anita was utterly astonished by what was unfolding.

Eric's emails to her revealed him to be a man she didn't know. Anita, as Delinquent Diana, told him that her husband was working away on an oil rig that she was lonely, and that they had increasingly less in common. Divorce was in the cards. Her ability to lie surprised her.

Eric, as he liked to be called, described his wife as someone who didn't turn him on. She was a good wife he wrote, an excellent cook and hostess, socially good for him and the backbone of their business. Why should he leave his marriage? He'd had a mistress for several years and was sad when she'd left Santa Barbara. He was "...interviewing for a new one." Anita almost choked.

With Daniel in the next room emailing her in real time, it was very hard not to confront him then and there. Interviewing for a new one? Her anger had reached a point where she, Anita, had a plan. She needed to remain very composed. Taking deep breaths she began to calm down, she had to formulate her plan. She could hear 'The Pina Colada Song' running through her mind.

"I was tired of my lady, we'd been together too long

Like a worn out recording of a favorite song
So while she lay there sleepin' I read the paper in bed
And in the personal columns, there was this letter I read . . ."

Robert had written to her with a similar story of a marriage gone stale, but not as blatantly disrespectful as her husband's. Rob was becoming quite interesting in a morbid way. Anita asked about his preferences, and over the next few emails, she learned more than she cared to know about the matter of sadomasochism. Robert wanted someone he could dominate. *What is it with these guys?* Anita thought over her coffee.

Robert wanted to speak to Delinquent Diana, but this posed a problem. She had an intuition that this man would have the knowledge she needed to execute her plan for Daniel; and with that thought in mind, she took the next morning off to purchase and set up a disposable pay-as-you-go cell phone.

She kept up her emails with "Eric" on a daily basis, while at the same time talking to Robert. These conversations were becoming a true confession of all manner of his deviant behaviors. He had recently lost his mistress as well, or subservient as he began to call her. His mistress had a daughter who was most unwell, so she had no more time for their liaisons. He was eager to find another. *Good help is hard to find*, Anita mused darkly. At times she listened with her mouth open as Robert told her that he and his mistress had used "toys." *Oh, my God*, she'd thought. *Dare I ask what toys?*

Anita was on a steep learning curve. She had decided to keep Rob for the time being. She wanted to pick his brains. She would need to be up-to-date about such deviant practices when she wrote to "Eric".

Eric was becoming increasing interested in Delinquent

Diana, or DD, as he now called her; he wanted a phone number. DD wrote him that this was impossible; she was afraid she'd be found out, that he'd recognize her voice. She told him her daughter was very savvy with cell phone and computing technology and would be sure to spot her. Eric accepted this but pushed for a time soon when they could meet. To Anita's horror, Eric told DD that his wife was going to San Luis Obispo for a weekend next month and he would have the Santa Barbara house to himself. DD was invited to spend the weekend in *her* house... in *her* bed so it seemed. Eric had described *their* bedroom in great detail in his efforts to lure DD.

What irony, thought Anita. Eric had sent her photos of himself. Anita had seen *her* husband in a photo *she* had taken. Daniel told DD where he lived; Anita felt shocked and vulnerable. Still, she said nothing, went on with day-to-day cooking and working normally, reading each day in the emails how distasteful she was to Daniel. There were some nights when she could barely look at her husband.

Rob told her how he would love to have her as his subservient. He suggested she call him M.R., an abbreviation for Master Robert. She'd rolled her eyes when she read this. Anita had been researching these practices online, and was surprised to see how common they were. It appeared to be a booming industry. Rob had told her he would like her to wear a dog collar if they were to be together. What did she think? Delinquent Diana said she thought it would be "erotic," and Rob fell in love that instant. He told her about the blindfolds she would wear to heighten her pleasure and add to the level of submission. How he, as her "father," would have to spank her, for her own good.

Anita was soon knowledgeable about the various paraphernalia of bondage that M.R. said were at his fingertips. He told her about the upcoming Folsom Street Fair in San Francisco, and invited her attend with him. He sent her a link, which read:

"FOLSOM SREET FAIR THE WORLD'S BIGGEST LEATHER EVENT." Bigger IS better at this 'only in San Francisco' event! With 400,000 fetish enthusiasts spread out over 12 city blocks, there is something for everyone. Located in historical Folsom Street, leather and fetish players from all over the world converge. With over 200 exhibitor booths showcasing fetish gear and toys, it's a pig's dream. Check out our massive live stage with top-name indie, electronic and alternative acts, our two huge dance areas, spinning underground EDM, public play stations, and an erotic artist's area with a sick and twisted performance stage. And, yes, you can still be naked, so avail yourself of our coat and clothes check areas as well...."

Anita had read and learned enough. When Rob told her he liked to have threesomes whenever possible, often hiring the extra, Delinquent Diana told him it was all too much for her. The risks involved with it all were far beyond her. Rob understood, though sadly, and was accepting. It seemed there were plenty of fish to be had in this quagmire of infidelity.

Anita turned a corner. Deciding she'd had enough of the cat and mouse games, she decided to take action. DD emailed Eric and asked him had he ever had any "naughty thoughts". Anita was over it all and she wanted a divorce, but being tidy by nature, she wanted to see this to a logical ending. She knew Daniel was full of hot air when it came to all this kinky stuff—albeit a philanderer.

However, Eric wrote back saying he did indeed have naughty thoughts and what did she have in mind. Anita was disgusted; she thought she'd give Daniel something to think about. "Dear Eric, I had such naughty thought about you while I was getting dressed this morning. I was wondering how my newly showered and soft pink bottom might feel after a spanking". Anita sat back and waited for her husband's response.

His response floored her. "Wow, very daring indeed. I like that you dare to try new things. Hmm, now that does sound good," he wrote back. Anita was stunned.

She rose to it and parried, "Wow, spanking! Do you really like this?"

Eric replied almost immediately, "I spanked my last submissive regularly. I enjoyed it very much as it was good for confirming our respective positions in the relationship. It shows clearly who the dominant is, and who's the sub. She loved it too, it made her feel comfortable and in her place. It's not that sensual, per se," Eric wrote, "but it does create that special bond."

Anita was speechless... sub... relationship... dominant... her Daniel?

Delinquent Diana wrote back, "I am excited by your response. How long have you been into all this? Have you ever been to The Folsom Street Fair?"

Eric was quick to reply: "I've been into the 'lifestyle' for almost twenty years and of course I've been to The Folsom Street Fair, I never miss it." Anita recoiled in white fury, recalling Daniel's business trips to San Francisco each September. "Time out for the boys", he'd said at the time. "Why don't you have a few days at the spar?"

Anita continued reading Eric's email. "Now that I know how naughty you are, I can't wait to meet you. I want you to follow my lead, accept my opinion of you and, for once, ignore your own self-opinion, and self-judgments. I want to be your master, oh mistress mine."

Anita was aghast. Her marriage was a fiasco. Her husband had no desire for her, but plenty for these deviant women, who would come and, according to Eric, *had* come into her home every time she'd been away. Why didn't she see it? Their housekeeper was very through, but surely there would have been some evidence. She felt sick and betrayed.

She wrote one more email to Eric. "Would you want to

own my mind? My body? What would you have me do? Is this what you and your former sub would do?"

She went home and cooked a large meal. An image of a last supper floated through her mind like a hideous gondola.

Over dinner she told Daniel she was going to spend the following week at their home in San Luis Obispo. Daniel remarked she looked pale and that he thought she could do with the break. He might travel with a friend to Morro Bay and then join her on Sunday. Or he might go shooting with another friend in the Mojave Desert, time for the boys to play with their toys. He wasn't sure yet. Anita said little, and Daniel took this to be approval. She didn't inquire about his friend.

The next morning Eric had written a long email. He told DD he wanted to possess her. He elaborated on his long-time interest in dominance and revealed he had always had a mistress, a subservient with whom he met regularly in the past. Eric said there were a few days ahead when he could be alone with her; he'd love to meet her and couldn't wait to play with her. He asked if she could come to Morro Bay the following weekend. DD said she would be there. Eric wrote back saying he would bring some toys. Nothing too much, some handcuffs, a light whip to get started. He said he could hardly contain himself; that his libido was rampant. He told DD the name of the motel, and the room number. Anita was both livid and excited.

Anita took a call the next day from one of the agencies her company served on along the Central Coast; she'd anticipated such a call. *"One of our regular nurses is sick, could you send one in place?"*

Anita said she could. She would do this shift herself and then head for Morro Bay. She needed to pick up some supplies. As a registered nurse, working a shift here and there in a nursing home, she had ready access to insulin.

The drive to Morro Bay was uneventful. Anita wrote a

checklist of what she needed to do. A sardonic smirk fluttered over her face as she imagined Daniel packing his toys. The smirk began to change; her eyes filled with tears. She turned on the CD player in her car, immersing herself in her music and the intermittent voice of the navigator that would direct her to the address of the motel Daniel/Eric had stipulated.

When Daniel opened the door of the motel to let DD in, he held out his arms. "Let me see you. My, but what long hair you have," simpered Daniel.

All the better to strangle you with, thought Anita as she walked into the room. "So, where are your toys?" she said in a cold voice.

Daniel realized he had been duped; his expression changed from that of shock to that of anger then laughter. He took the remote for the television and sat on the end of the bed, surfing through channels and shaking with laughter at her. Hysterical laughter. "You pathetic bitch," he said with his back to her.

Anita took the wrench out of her coat pocket.

Paul Alan Fahey

Paul Alan Fahey is the author of the *Lovers and Liars* gay wartime romance series—a 2014 finalist for a Rainbow Award. He is the editor of the 2013 Rainbow Award-winning nonfiction anthology, *The Other Man: 21 Writers Speak Candidly About Sex, Love, Infidelity, &Moving On.* His short fiction has appeared in *Byline, Palo Alto Review, Long Story Short, African American Review, The MacGuffin, Thema, Gertrude, Kaleidoscope*, and in various anthologies from *Cup of Comfort, My Mom's My Hero,* to *The Best of SLO NightWriters in Tolosa Press 2009-2013,* and *Somewhere in Crime.* He lives on the California Central Coast with his husband, Robert Franks, and a gaggle of shelties.

How "Red Mesa" came about: Every morning on my way to work in Santa Maria, I crossed over the bridge from San Luis to Santa Barbara County. Off to my right on the edge of the Nipomo mesa, I noticed a home with a red tile roof and wondered who lived in this seemingly isolated spot. I did quite a bit of what-ifing and suddenly a story idea materialized with these three components: a woman with a history of abuse, a murder, and justice served.

Red Mesa
by
Paul Alan Fahey

Why was I going to see Letty? I couldn't say for sure, but somehow I was

drawn to the white stucco house with the red tile roof. After all these years, I still had my suspicions. Maybe I just wanted to know the truth.

I turned off 101 and stopped for the light at the Antique Warehouse—the one painted bright pink next to the SUV dealer with an inflated Godzilla on its roof. The signal changed, and I headed west along the arroyo.

The wind was dry and a bit cool for an October afternoon, and I sensed the

fog hovering in the distance. I shifted gears when the road began to wind up the mesa and left the sprawl of Santa Maria behind me.

I'd first met Letty back in the seventies. She'd called the office, and I'd driven out to see her in Nipomo. One of her boarders, a Mr. Hathaway, had gone missing. He was an eighty-something gent and one of my clients at Central Coast Social Services. I was head of the department back then, but I'm now retired.

"Hathaway packed his belongings and drove off in the middle of the night,"

she'd said, then she pointed back down the road I'd just traveled. "That-a-way."

At Letty's ranch style home, I parked the car, went down the walk, pushed the front doorbell, and waited.

There was no answer so I walked around back and found her in the garden. She seemed smaller and shrunken, different from that last day in court. The brim of her hat hid her face. Her shoes were encrusted with mud. Bending over a scraggly fern with a pair of shears in her hand, she had the stance of a woman who'd learned early on that life was anything but a bowl of cherries.

"The sand's bad this time of year," she said. "It shifts in the wind. All I can do is plant, feed, and water them, then hope for the best."

The hum of a yellow bi-plane on a sightseeing tour of the Oceano Dunes caught Letty's attention. The word "RIDES" was written in black letters on the bottom of one of the wings. She stood up, slipped the shears into her apron pocket, and cupped a hand over her eyes. "Maybe it's Hathaway, checking me out to see if I'm still alive."

"Or his ghost," I said. "Haunting you."

"Why are you here?" She came toward me.

"Just a visit," I said. "Nothing more. I was—"

"Curious?"

"Maybe."

"I don't take people in any more," she said. "You saw to that. You and the endless parade of social workers, poking their noses where they shouldn't. The police found no evidence. Why weren't you satisfied?"

"Letty, it was my—"

"Job? I know. All that fuss over one elderly fellow who lost his mind and ran off."

"I was responsible. I signed the form that placed him in your care."

"Care. That's what I do. Did. Nursed them, cared for them when no one wanted them. They were old, sick, and then they died. That's what happens. It's called life."   She walked away and went back to her gardening. The hair was grayer now, her face thinner with more crevices than a relief map of the Sierras. She walked with a limp and a slight shaking motion as if she had a pebble in her shoe and was trying to dislodge it.

I sat on the patio, watched her pour water from a can onto the parched earth. She cut off a small piece of wire mesh and made a little fence around the young plants to keep away the deer that roamed the mesa at night.

I walked to the cliff. The fog swept in across the arroyo and crept up the bluff. I knew the sea was out there, a few miles to the west.

Letty finished her planting and joined me. We didn't speak for some time, just stood there, gazing off into the distance.

"You won't leave till I tell you."

It wasn't a question so I didn't answer her. Perhaps she needed a father confessor, someone to share her secret. I didn't work at Central anymore. Who would I tell?

"I was thirteen years old," she said, "on my way home from school when it

happened."

I let her talk. Neither of us was in a hurry.

"The school's gone now. But it wasn't far from here." She pointed south to the other side of the riverbed. "I remember the wind. Like today, cool but dry, with the leaves turning overhead and the fog everywhere. So thick I didn't see him standing by the road till he was practically on top of me."

She paused, gave a little laugh that ended in a cough. "Bad choice of

words." She went on. "The man said my father was ill and, of course, I believed him. I got in his car and you can guess the rest. They discovered me that night, Papa and

Enrique, a migrant who worked in our fields. I was badly bruised and unconscious. They never found the man."

"But you did."

"Yes."

"Hathaway."

"Wrinkled and worn out, but I knew it was him. The voice. Not something I was likely to forget. Ever." Letty shivered and drew her sweater up around her shoulders. She was winding down. "I don't know why I'm so talkative. Must be your charm."

"But how...where?"

She looked down at the ice plant, ran the toe of her shoe over its crimson blossoms that spread under her feet and spilled over the bluff like tiny drops of blood.

It was then I understood.

I went back to the chair and picked up my coat. "Maybe I'll come again, see how those plants are doing?"

"Why bother? You got what you came for," and then she turned away, did that little hop-skip I'd noticed earlier before she disappeared inside the house.

Minutes later, I was stopped at the light by the pink palace I mentioned

earlier, near the 101 southbound entrance. I looked up at Godzilla, at the poorly drawn features, the misshapen head, the sun-bleached colors, and I knew Letty was right. I wouldn't be back. I was no longer curious.

Lani Steele

Lani Steele has a divided spirt: part in her native California, part in Kaua'i where she would live if she could, and part in perpetual motion around the world. She has lived in several countries including Chad, is published in poetry, mystery fiction, and non-fiction, and recently retired from 53 years as an educator. She lives in Los Osos with her husband Gary. Their four children are far-flung and require many visits.

There is an unsolved murder of a young woman who was found in Montana de Oro in the 1970's (I believe). The story haunts me, so I wrote a solution for myself. Kaia is projected as a series character, with stories on the Central Coast and on Kaua'i. The introductory story, A DARK AND BROODING HONEYMOON, is set in the Kalaulau Valley on Kaua'i and touches on the legend of the hermit of Kalaulau.

Seance Is Believing

She was here today. It's the second time I've seen her. The ceanothus are blue and smell like gas flames. Like the last time....
* * *
<u>2007, Harddick</u>: Lt. Richard Hardwick, 50, graying at the temples, more flesh than muscle, was called Harddick by his fellow detectives. Had been for more than twenty years.

and probably would be until he retired. And despite his wife Jolene's deep sighs and sometimes derisive snorts, he wasn't planning to retire anytime soon. He loved his job; he wasn't finished yet. Not until he saw Mary's murderer get what he deserved. He knew the man. All the detectives knew who had killed Mary. They'd just never been able to prove it.

Mary Larkton, 23, dead of strangulation, January, 1977. Found by horrified hikers on a narrow trail amidst the blue-flowering ceanothus, twisted, her head at an impossible angle. All around her, the blues and greens of sky, tiny flowers, and the low scrub brush of our California hills. Below, a cold, brilliant green winter sea stretched away westward, to the land of the dead.

Richard Hardwick grew up in these hills and the nearby Los Osos Valley, on the gentle coastlands of Central California. It was a safe place to grow up. To keep it that way, Hardwick joined the Sheriff's Department in 1969, after his tour in 'Nam. There were few deputies and vast areas to cover, but crimes were few and murder rare. Not like today's drug labs and gang members all over the county. In 1977, murders like Mary's weren't supposed to happen. *And maybe,* Hardwick reflected, *it was because we couldn't imagine it that we couldn't solve it. Except…we know, dammit, we know. That's why I'm sitting here, under a bush, expecting the killer to return to the scene of the crime.*

Detective Hardwick shifted his weight from left to right buttock, his legs stretched uncomfortably in front of him, his back hurting from sitting for two hours with only the support of a tall shrub. His nose ran, his eyes watered. No one had come down the trail during the time he'd been observing this spot, the place where Mary's body had been sprawled twenty years before.

* * *

2007, Kaia: The old mare found her way down the trail with increasing confidence, despite her almost total blindness. I began to relax and look around. It was good to be back on the coast again. I love this landscape of rocky hills and fertile valleys, wave-worn cliffs and sculpted sand dunes. Despite all the new houses and the loss of hundreds of eucalyptus to builders' bulldozers, it was still a magnificent view.

"Go take a ride, Kaia," Tracy had urged. "Honey needs the exercise and it's a perfect day. We can talk when you get back." She'd glanced at her mother, Melly, clearly signaling: *When she's gone.*

Honey was a sweet-tempered bay mare who had been traveling these hillsides since long before I had seen them. Tracy rescued the mare from a brutal owner when she was in high school. All during our college days at Cal Poly in nearby San Luis Obispo, Honey had carried us over hills and dunes, away from exams, books, horny professors and stodgy boyfriends. We rode to the edge of the sea, for which we shared the passion of those raised near it—she in Los Osos, I in Kaua'i.

I'd returned to San Luis Obispo to give some background lectures and make final arrangements for an adventure tour of Hawai'i I was to lead for Cal Poly professors and their spouses. I'm Kaia Malama, of Kaua'i and San Luis Obispo, independent travel consultant, Hawaiian/Chinese American, and divorced mother of Aloha, the cutest six-year-old in the Northern Hemisphere. I was in the middle of putting together a very satisfactory mix of hidden trails, petroglyphs, and mummies, balanced with soaking in natural hot pools and sleeping on pikaki-scented pillows at antique-filled bed and breakfast inns, when Tracy called and begged me for help.

"I heard how you found that hermit guy on Kaua'i. And I remember how you solved the dorm thefts when we were at Poly. You've got a knack. And I need you. My mom... my aunt..." Tracy hadn't been able to continue. After knowing her for over fifteen years, that was the first time I'd heard her speechless. So I drove out to Los Osos, to find Tracy strangely evasive and very anxious to put me on a horse.

Honey snorted and edged sideways into the chaparral, rousing me from my reverie. That was good, because the next thing she did was jump straight up and two feet over, coming down trembling and prancing in a manner surprisingly lively for such an old and docile horse. She was snorting and backing up and I needed all of my modest horsemanship skills to stay on. Suddenly, a tall shrub reared up in front of us. Honey jumped again, then bucked. I made a nice arc in the air and landed at the feet of the shrub, cursing. Honey took off. The shrub said angrily, "That damned horse almost stepped on my balls."

I didn't know what kind of man was posing as a ceanothus. Suspecting the man was up to no good, I didn't want to find out. It was a perfect spot for mischief: two trails came together, with the large flowering shrubs at their junction. He could see up and down both trails, who was coming, and if they were alone. One person would be child's play for this big man, especially with the advantage of surprise. Honey had dashed off down the trail, where she waited about a hundred yards away, watching me and the talking bush nervously. I began backing away from him, scooting on my behind, ignoring his outstretched hand.

"Are you hurt?" the man asked, brushing the leaves and twigs from his flannel shirt and jeans, and offering his hand again.

"No, no thanks to you," I had decided on a brisk offensive. "What are you doing hiding in the bushes like that? That'd spook any horse. Are you some kind of naturalist?" I thought I'd give him a plausible excuse for what seemed an inexcusable activity, while I edged toward Honey. Then I'd make a dash for it.

"Harddick... er, Hardwick, Richard," the big man actually stammered a bit, holding out a hand in which his Sheriff's Department badge shone like a small sun. I breathed easier. I'd worked with the sheriffs before—his badge looked genuine.

"No, I... there was... sometimes I just come out here to think things over," he finished lamely, obviously having no intention of telling me what he'd actually been doing. "Jolene, my wife, she gets messages from... well, you know, she says from spirits. One of them predicted something might happen. Of course," he straightened himself ramrod tall, looked me directly in the eye and asserted, "there's nothing to it, but once in a while she's right, so I thought I might as well think things over out here as at my desk." His look dared me to deny the perfect rationality of his explanation.

I was silent, a rare occurrence. After a few seconds he said, "Isn't that Honey? I heard she was blind."

"She is, but she knows the trails. However, walking, talking bushes are not in her memory bank. How do you know Honey?"

Hardwick ignored this and walked down the trail, clucking softly to Honey, who walked calmly up to him and nuzzled his pockets. He pulled out a sugar cube, gave it to her, and led her to where I stood.

"Sorry about that. Looks like you're not hurt. Here's your horse." And he walked away.

"Don't worry, I can get on without a hand up," I called after him. He never looked back. His neck was scarlet.

* * *

Tracy laughed when I told her about the encounter. "He actually said, 'Harddick'?", she asked. "Supposedly they only use that name inside the Department. He likes to look tough, but as you can tell by the sugar in his pocket, he's really soft-hearted. Jolene runs him around by the nose. We've known them forever. They live out on the county road, near where I found Honey."

"Does Jolene converse with spirits?" I asked.

"She's a channeler and a psychic," replied Tracy. "She started with the spirits of Chumash Indians and Spaniards on the old ranch where they live. But she's actually helped the local police and sheriff's departments solve some cases. She told them where to look for Luisa Alvares, the little kidnapped girl, and they found her alive. The cops are still skeptical for the most part, but they try her when everything else fails. But, she can't work on demand. It's more that sometimes things come to her. Like..." She stopped, looking so unlike my cheerful friend that I felt as though I'd seen her ghost. Tracy is a freckled redhead, tall and big-boned, who usually radiates competence and cheer. Now she looked pale and uncertain.

"Like what?"

"Like why I asked you here," Tracy got up and poured us tea, her large hands trembling. "Jolene has been hearing from Mary. Mary is warning my mom. Jolene has visions, seeing someone falling. I don't know whether to pooh-pooh it or what to do. Mom's acting tough, even though I know she's spooked. Then the notes came, and so now Mom's worried for both herself and me, and Jax is furious and keeping a loaded gun handy. Mom wants *me* to leave town, which of course I won't do, and another of those damned notes came today." Unable to go on, Tracy had tears running down her face.

I had known Tracy and her mom Melly long enough to piece together most of this disjointed account. Melly had been through a lot. Twenty years before, her sister Mary had gone out one day to walk in Montana de Oro, the state park where I'd been riding Honey, a beautiful land of cliffs, copses, and coves much cherished by the locals. Mary never came back. Her body was found on the trail, strangled. The killer was never found. Melly was shattered, but in time put her life together, eventually divorcing Tracy's father, and after Tracy moved into dorms at Cal Poly, moving in with her lover, Jax. Melly and Jax had opened Reader's Roost Bookstore which has been supporting them modestly for the past several years.

Tracy's childhood had been shadowed by Mary's murder. The unsuccessful hunt for Mary's killer was followed for several years by Melly's obsessive protectiveness toward Tracy. Finally, therapy and time had allowed their relationship to take a more positive course. But now Mary's shadow was again cast over their lives, her spirit supposedly speaking to and through Jolene Hardwick. What I didn't follow was the part about notes.

"What notes?" I asked. Tracy opened the drawer of her mother's desk and thrust two grubby pieces of lined school paper into my hand. The notes were printed in block letters. The first one said:

I SEEN YOU. I KNEW YOU COME BACK. I WILL MEET YOU AT THE REGULER PLAISE.

The second read: WHY DIDN'T YOU COME? I AM WATING. I SEE YOU.

"Yuck," I said. "These came to Melly? How were they delivered?"

"That's the creepy part," Tracy said. "Someone pushed them through the mail slot. She glanced at the slot, protected by a little metal hood on the outside, which had allowed the note-deliverer's hand to come part way into their home, and their lives.

"I need help, Kaia. We've got to find out who's sending these. Is it the killer? Is it just some sick crank? Do you think Mary is really warning Melly? If my Mom's in danger, we've got to get her out of here. But she refuses to leave. She says he already wrecked her life once, she won't let him do it again."

"Have you shown these to the Sheriff's detectives?"

"Melly won't let me."

I thought about Lt. Hardwick, waiting under a bush. Was he still waiting for Mary's killer?

"Can you help, Kaia?" Tracy implored.

I had some time before I had to leave with my tour, but I had other concerns. One was Aloha. I had left her in Lihue, Kauai's main township, with my go-go businesswoman mother, who did not fancy life as a baby-sitter. Luckily, Aloha had my Uncle Kimo to walk her to and from school, spoil her with Hawaiian crackseed, and tell her bedtime stories. The second reservation was a natural reluctance, inherited from both my Chinese and my Hawaiian ancestors, to meddle with the spirits of the departed. We have a healthy respect for the dead and don't want to disturb them unnecessarily. One of the reasons I lead the tours in Hawaii is to be sure that respect is paid to the resting places of our dead, something that many tourists don't know or care about.

"Kaia!" Tracy interrupted my conversation with myself.

"Let's see what we can find out while I'm here. Then I'll see whether I need to come back." I explained my concerns to Tracy. She went to her mother's desk again and, from a cupboard on one side, she pulled out a scrapbook. Without a word, she opened it to pictures of her mother and Mary, young girls, riding the Irish Hills behind Los Osos. Melly and Mary on the beach in Morro Bay with Morro Rock dramatic behind them. Mary and Melly graduating from high school, then from Cal Poly. Melly as bride, Mary as maid of honor. An article about Mary's work as an art therapist at local prisons and juvenile centers. And then pages and pages of clippings about Mary's murder, the investigation, and then, blank pages.

"OK, Trace," I sighed. "I'll stay until we get to the bottom of this, or as close as we can. *But,* we have to tell the Sheriffs Department. And you may have to go to Kaua'i and save Aloha from the Tiny Tycoon," as I called my mother, whose goal was to own Kaua'i before she died.

Tracy hugged me fiercely and went to make more tea. I read the clipping closely, then went to phone Lt. Richard Hardwick to tell him I knew what he was doing under that ceanothus, and to invite him out to coffee.

* * *

Harddick was not anti-feminist. He was too smart for that. He knew too many smart women for that. But sometimes, dammit, he wished women would pretend, the way they used to, that they weren't as smart as they are.

"Shit!" he slammed the phone down.

"What?" his colleague, Tutoy, asked.

"I have to go to coffee with a gorgeous young woman," Harddick growled, "who seems to know my business better than I do myself."

Tutoy, a small, wiry Filipino of rumored prodigious sexual proclivities, offered to take his place, but Harddick was on his way out the door. He swung his unmarked car out of the lot in front of the Sheriff's station/jail, along the two-lane road which wound in deceptively bucolic nonchalance to the juvenile hall and then past the dog pound. At Highway 1 he took the right into San Luis Obispo.

She was at a table in an upscale coffee shop in the center of town. Even in a town full of nubile coeds, well-dressed professional women, and well-kept wives, she stood out: about 5′7″, slim and straight, with amber skin, almond eyes, and about three feet of lustrous black hair hanging to her waist. She was sipping ginger tea. When she saw Hardwick, she beckoned to the androgynous waitperson to bring a menu. The detective eased into a chair that seemed too fragile for him, waved the menu away, and ordered coffee and berry pie.

Kaia wasted no time. "You were staking out the site of Mary Larkton's murder," she asserted. "Why? Is the killer still around? Is he active?"

Hardwick also wasted no time on amenities. "Let's see the notes," he demanded. "Then we'll talk."

Kaia was reluctant to show him the notes. Although she felt somehow she could trust him, the notes were Melly's. They were scary. And they were all Kaia had to bargain with. But she had to start somewhere. Pulling the crumpled papers from her purse, she smoothed them on the table in front of him.

"No possibility of getting prints from these?" she asked.

"He probably was clever enough not to leave any." Hardwick replied. "Not to mention how many hands they've been through by now. But we can try. I'll keep them?"

Kaia appreciated his asking instead of telling. She nodded. "So do you have an idea who wrote these? Do you think it's the same guy? I assume it's a man?"

She turned one of the notes. "It's school paper. My daughter Aloha does her homework on paper like this. Could it possibly be a teacher?"

"It's still an open investigation, Ms. Malama." The detective, non-commital, concentrated on his pie.

"Call me Kaia," she said. "I know that the case is still open, and you can't tell me much, but Tracy and her mother are terrified. Can't you tell us you're working on it with some assurance of nailing this creep? Is he local? Do you think he's done other murders? Is he obsessive? There's no record of similar unsolved cases in this area. I know. I checked the newspaper files."

Hardwick spared her a grudging, pie-stained grin of acknowledgement. "You did your homework." He pulled an envelope from his jacket pocket and drew several news clippings from it, spreading them on top of the odious notes. The clippings described the strangling deaths of three young women between 23 and 31. The murders had taken place, according to the articles, in Half-Moon Bay, Samoa Township, and Moss Landing, all coastal California towns strikingly similar to our local area. The first clipping detailed a murder five years after Mary's, the second five years later, and the third fifteen years after Mary was found—five years ago.

"Oh, my God," Kaia breathed. "You do know who did this," she tried not to sound accusatory.

"Knowing and proving are two different things," Hardwick tried not to sound defensive. He felt defensive. All the guys who'd been on this case were angry at not being able to nail the guy, even though they were pretty sure who he was. The killer was either very clever or very lucky, killing and moving on. Always women alone in lonely places.

"Anyway," he said to Kaia, "those clippings are Jolene's, not the Department's."

"So what do we do now?" Kaia asked, setting her teacup down briskly.

"*We* don't do anything. *I'll* try to get a watch on Melly's place, but we're way undermanned. Maybe that's what you could do, try to see who comes to the door with another of those love notes."

Kaia was angry at being shut out so effectively, but she stood, smoothed her skirt, and held out her hand to Hardwick. "Thank you, Detective, for your help," she said sweetly and with clear irony.

"Goddamn it! I've been on this case twenty years! You think I don't want this guy?" Several diners craned their necks to see who was yelling.

Kaia sat down again. "Then let me help. How about your wife? You said she was in contact with Mary, true? Remember, I'm not such a sceptic. My people talk to their dead all the time." She smiled.

"Shit," said Hardwick. "Sorry. I don't know whether there's anything to it or not. There's guys in the Department swear by Jolene. But they never hear her goin' on about when she was a priestess of the Goddess and I was a slave. I'm real tired of that story."

"But," prompted Kaia.

"But," he went on, "she did help find that kid. And she has helped on several lesser cases. But this one, I don't know. It's too close to home. She knows how much I want this guy."

"So you think maybe it's wishful channeling?" she asked.

"Something like that. Except, it's not clear, and she's real upset whenever this Mary comes through. She never seems to get much. Last night, she had a few of the regulars in, folks who sort of check in with their relatives on the other side every so often. Right in the middle of Meg Sweeney's great-grandmother, Mary breaks in, says, 'He's here! He's here! Tell Melly!' But then she's gone before Jo knows just what to tell Melly. Who's here?"

"You think it's him—the killer?"

"That would be handy, wouldn't it?" the detective smiled wearily, and Kaia thought how he looked a bit like her Uncle Kimo. "But we don't know and Mary's gone back to wherever she goes. Jolene doesn't know whether to tell Melly or not. That poor woman's been through enough. She did tell Tracy, but I don't know if Tracy's told her mom."

"She has," Kaia said. "May I talk to Jolene?"

"Jolene talks to who she wants to. Call her and ask." Hardwick scribbled a number on the back of his business card.

"I'll be in touch." Kaia rose again. She looked purposeful and, Hardwick thought, like a cat who sees, far off, the canary she's planning to eat for dinner. While he was musing about her intentions, Kaia picked up the check, paid it at the counter, waved to Hardwick, and exited. *Stalking,* he thought.

* * *

I found Tracy at her mother's apartment, having a glass of wine with Melly and Jax. And going through boxes of old stuff. Although Trace had found a new apartment, she had delayed moving from Melly's place since the advent of the notes. Also, Tracy had no furniture. The three of them were sorting out the contents of the boxes to see what Tracy might be able to use. She had set aside a funky old map of Los Osos in the 1930's and a couple of her high school yearbooks.

"Melly, does old Mrs.Wanita still live next door? And does she still monitor the entire neighborhood from her window?" I asked, accepting a glass of local chardonnay.

"Yes," Jax and Melly answered together. And Jax continued, "What a pain! She actually reported us for having two garbage cans instead of one. Luckily, we're approved for two. Really pissed old Wanna-be off."

"Let's give her a job," I proposed. And they agreed that putting Mrs. Wanita on the payroll (for a few paperbacks) would be a good way to get free surveillance of all and sundry who came to their door.

"Let's even give her that old camera of mine," Jax offered. She'll love it, and if it works, we'll have a picture. Do you really think the guy is nuts enough to come back in broad daylight?"

"He's done it twice before," Tracy pointed out. "No notes in the morning, and notes when you get home. Maybe he pays a kid to drop them off."

"Sherlock Wanita will find out for us." Melly looked a great deal more cheerful, and toasted her snoopy neighbor with more of the excellent wine. Flushed, she looked more like Tracy's sister than her mother. They shared the redhead coloring, although Melly's was more auburn to Tracy's flaming red. Melly was also more petite than either her sister or her daughter.

After Melly and Jax took off for family-style Mexican food at La Casita, Tracy continued exploring the storage boxes while I called Jolene and made an appointment for the following afternoon. "She'd like you to come," I said, covering the mouthpiece. "Do you think you could? It might help, she says."

Tracy made a little pout of distaste, then decided. "If it'll help, I'll do it," she agreed. "Look what I found under Melly's old letterman's sweater."

She held up some old recordings the sisters had made years ago. Tracy waved the old-fashioned 78's over her head. "Thank God Jax made Mom keep this old record player. They still listen to LPs." We listened for a few minutes to Mary and Melly, around 1975, singing, giggling, speaking their dreams onto a scratchy disk. Mary had a low, strong, vibrato voice, easily distinguishable from Melly's melodic soprano. She didn't sound at all dead.

* * *

Hardwick and his wife lived in an old farm house on a rise above a sharp curve in the old county road. Behind a picket fence, a flower garden showed a profusion of pansies, impatiens, and a few early narcissus. Jolene was a big woman with bright blond hair and a strong handshake. She wore jeans and a hand-knit sweater with cats on it. She greeted the girls, went off to stir something delicious-smelling in the kitchen, then called them into the capacious, old-fashioned dining room. She shut the kitchen door, pulled heavy drapes over the windows, and invited them to sit at the highly polished oak table. On a sideboard behind her, a set of Italian peasant dishes were splashes of color in the dark room.

"So, Dick's told you about Mary. I knew her, you know. I was older than her, of course, but everyone knew everyone in this town at one time. Real nice girl. Bit of a loner, but not anti-social, you know what I mean? She just liked to be alone sometimes. Anyways, she had a boyfriend and Dick and the guys grilled him good, but he had an alibi. He was in class at Cal Poly at the time of the murder. Thirty people around him. And no one could have *acted* as upset as he was. Left town the next year, after he graduated. Lives up north now."

I was distracted, thinking about the boyfriend, while Jolene explained the difficulties of summoning spirits on demand. I was aware of Tracy's voice explaining their urgency, almost pleading. Then I heard a new voice, a voice that caused prickles to crawl up my spine. It was Mary's voice. Jolene was stiff in her chair, and from her mouth Mary was saying, "Tell Mel... he's here. Behind her.... watch... Har... it's him! He'll hurt... *No*, Harl..."

Tracy gasped. I took her hand.

Jolene was shaking and tears ran from her eyes which looked at nothing. Then, without much transition, she looked at us calmly. "She came, didn't she?" Jolene asked.

"Did she say enough to help?" She took a tissue from her sweater sleeve and wiped her eyes.

Tracy looked dazed. "I think so, but I can't believe it. I have to talk to my mom. My God, if it's him… he's been here all this time. All those kids…"

"Harley?" Jolene asked. Tracy jumped.

"Did Mary tell you?" she asked.

Jolene was up, pulling the drapes open. "I hate the dark. I hope someday I can leave these open all day. But, dead or not, everyone seems to have something to say. And I seem to be the spiritual AT&T in this neck of the woods. Can I get you some coffee?"

Tracy's freckles stood out in her pale face. I nodded to Jolene, who bustled out and returned with a tray of cookies, a pot of coffee, real cream and brown sugar. Then she answered the question that was still hanging in the air.

"No, honey. They talk through me, but not to me. But, I've had a feelin' about that feller for a long time. And when Mary showed up, she wanted to tell, I think, but she was waitin' for you. Drink some coffee, honey," she pushed a cup towards Tracy, who took it and drank gratefully. She looked better.

"It is spooky, though," Jolene said, "him working at the school and all. He's a custodian at the old grammar school," she explained to me.

I admired Jolene's calm manner and down-to-earth acceptance of her unusual gift. And I particularly admired the way in which Jolene didn't ask a lot of questions. Must be a great trait in a cop's wife, I thought, which reminded me of Hardwick's remarks.

Hoping to distract Tracy, I asked Jolene, "Is it true you were a priestess of the Goddess long ago, and Lt. Hardwick was a slave?"

Jolene chuckled, "I tell him that to keep him in line. He knows that. Just likes to complain. Actually, I haven't had any past life revelations. But it only seems fair for him to wait on me once in a while."

Tracy's grin was my reward for being nosy. We thanked Jolene and drove the winding road west, into the setting sun, an orange disk swathed in pink and purple clouds which reflected off ponds and windmill blades like a Cubist painting.

"I think I know something we can do to get this guy," said Tracy.

"Me, too," I replied, as we parked in front of Melly's. "but for today, *pau hana*. No more work. Let's go to La Casita, I'm starving."

* * *

She's coming to meet me. She smiled at me last time I seen her. We'll be together. This time she won't say 'no'. She can't. I won't let her. Those other Marys said 'no'. But this is the right Mary. My Mary...

* * *

"I'm too nervous to eat," Tracy said, crumbling tortilla chips into fragments over her chili verde.

"I know," I agreed, scooping up the last of my refried beans with a chip. "But I must keep up my strength to defeat the forces of evil."

Tracy smiled wanly. "So far, evil seems to be winning, although it's strange to think of Harley as evil. He's always been kind of pitiable. Some people make fun of him, but Mary never did. And she wouldn't let us do it, either. She said he was an anachronism, the last of his line."

Harley Boissart's *line* had been locally prominent for over a hundred years. His family had owned vast tracts of land along the Central Coast, including the park in which

Mary was killed. But the family had died out, leaving most of the land as a gift to the State. Harley had a few acres, but he was too disorganized to farm it. He's made his modest living as a custodian at the oldest of our local elementary schools, Los Osos Grammar. The kids—and the teachers too, for that matter—thought he was 'weird.' But, in the old-fashioned way of small towns, he was accepted by most and protected by a few. He never bothered the children, although they sometimes teased him, pulling their pants way down around their hips the way Harley's always drooped, and imitating his bowlegged walk.

He lived on his land in a farmhouse so old no one could remember seeing it with paint on it, using only the kitchen and back porch as his living quarters. He liked to go to the old Sweet Springs Saloon in the evenings and schmooze with the other old timers from town, nursing a beer or two. As far as anyone knew, Harley had never had a lady friend. But once, twenty years ago, he had liked to walk with Mary, out at Montana de Oro. Many people had seen them together, but the ones who teased Harley often ended with split lips or black eyes. Harley didn't like being teased about Mary.

"What about Mary?" I asked Tracy. "She had a boyfriend. What was she doing with Harley?"

"She was just being kind to him. She said he was a lost spirit, like an old cowboy out of time. She'd listen to him go on and on. Apparently, he asked her to marry him. He thought he was going to sue the State, get the ranch back, and they'd live happily ever after."

"My God," I shivered. "She worked at the State Hospital for the criminally insane. Didn't she pick up on anything?"

"Later, we put things together. But she thought he was harmless, that she could handle him. She'd had training in self-defense at the Hospital. She was so sure of herself. But get this: his mother was a redhead named Mary, with whom he lived until she was ninety-eight. She finally died, leaving him nothing. Even the place he lives in belongs to the state, but he can live there until he dies. As long as he doesn't marry."

"That was in her will?" I asked incredulously.

"Yep," said Tracy. "But that all happened *after* Mary's murder. And when Mary was killed, the old woman swore that Harley was at home with her. So did Harley. So did the Chinaman."

"Chinaman?" I was too intrigued to take offense at the politically incorrect term.

"Yes, an old guy who worked on their land forever. Had no family. Stayed with the Boissarts from the day he arrived from Suchow until the day he died. Never learned much English. Well, you couldn't tell, really. He was mute. But he gestured at Harley and then at the clock: 'Harley home at time of killing.'"

"How convenient. I supposed he's dead now, too?"

"Probably," Tracy replied. "No one knows. He disappeared as soon as the old woman died. Stole her antique clock. Harley ranted about it for weeks."

"Do you really think," I asked, "that Harley is clever enough to disappear, find a girl named Mary who's a redhead several hundred miles from here and kill her, leaving no clues, every five years? And then come back here and act normal... or Harley-normal?"

"Yes," said Tracy simply. "He's obsessed. According to what I've read, these kinds of killer usually have to kill more and more. There are only four other murders that we know of that fit this pattern. But there could be more. Around here, people's animals disappear, too; often they're never seen again."

She shivered. "But even if he's getting crazier, isn't it an awful chance to stick notes right into someone's front-door mailbox? And why Mom? She's not a Mary, and her hair's more auburn than red. She does look a bit like Mary, though. You think he believes Mom is Mary?"

"Maybe. How often do you and your mom see him in a week, usually?" I asked.

Tracy thought. "Could be every day for a while, then not at all for a few days. You know are small towns are: the bank, the post office, the bakery, the coffee shop You see the same people over and over. He's seen her for years."

"Seeing Melly. But now he's seeing Mary, or something is making him think that he is. Does he come into the bookstore? Is your Mom nice to him?"

"He only ever comes once a year, to get an almanac. But Mom is always nice to him, because Mary was. He goes by and waves or sometimes they are in the diner at the same time and have a cup of coffee. But they've done that for years. Oh." She stopped in mid-flow. "It's five years again, isn't it? So now he thinks Mary has come back?"

"Yes," I said. "And in a way, she has. And we're her agents. So let's work on our plan. We've only got one chance to get Lt. Hardwick and his guys on our side, so let's not blow it."

* * *

Harddick hated it. He didn't like anything about their plan, from first to last. But they played their trump card— they'd do it anyway, with or without him or his men. And since the Sheriff's Department had never revealed suspicions of any named suspect, the girls figured that they couldn't get in trouble for interfering with an investigation. They'd claim ignorance. If they survived.

Harddick played hardball. He lied, he threatened, he cajoled. Then he gave in. He swore. He cursed all women, from the Goddess on down. Then he sat down with his men and planned.

* * *

It was a plan worthy of Jessica Fletcher. Just as simple, just as harebrained, just as dangerous. All we would do was send Melly out walking, down the trail Mary had walked, at the same time of day, wearing clothes as similar as possible to Mary's, with Mary's Dodgers baseball cap on backwards. Then we'd wait for Harley to make his move, and nab him in the act. We all knew that something could go horribly wrong, but Melly was adamant that she wanted to put an end to the terror of the notes and to the haunting ache of the past twenty years.

We decided we'd try the plan on a Saturday, when Harley wasn't working. We knew we might have to try for several Saturdays, that Melly might have to walk and talk with him daily as her sister had, until the trap was sprung. We knew we might not be fast enough to stop him in the act. But, as usual, it was what we didn't know that would hurt us.

Tracy and I went out on Honey on Thursday before the Saturday when we were going to try out the plan. We had to take turns riding, since the old mare couldn't carry us both at once. Without thinking or planning, we headed down the trail toward the spot where Mary's body had lain, where Honey had almost stepped on Hardwick. When we reached the spot, I was walking. I eyed the ceanothus suspiciously, and Honey snorted and pranced a bit, but no one was there. We went on down to the cliffs.

The scenery along the cliffs of Montana de Oro is one of the better-kept secrets of California. It has been used in movies to depict Maine and Cornwall. Rocky fingers of land reach out into a restless sea When the tide is out, seals and sea lions laze on exposed rocks, at home amid the surge and crash of water and the high laments of sea birds. When the tide is up, waves surge hungrily around the bottoms of the cliffs and blowing foam wets not only those on the edge, but anyone walking nearby. The tide was out today, and the wind and sea relatively calm. The ocean was the clear, glassy green that it only shows in winter. We strolled along a cliffside path, leading Honey, letting her graze along the way when she could find green weeds and grasses. The sun was warm on our faces.

It's all scrub brush in the fields along here, but it gets pretty high. There's the chaparral, and the ceanothus, and some grasses that grow tall during rainy season. It looks as though you could see anyone who was around, but there's actually plenty of cover. Only right along the edge of the cliffs is the path cleared. I was scanning the fields behind us, wondering if someone was watching. Harley was supposed to be at work, but still, it was scary to think that someone could be there. Because it was spoiling the beauty of the day, I tried to put those thoughts from my mind.

Tracy said, "Look. There's Coral Cove. Remember when we used to sunbathe topless down there? We were always scrambling for our tops because somebody always came along."

She was smiling at the memory of our escapades. I reminded her that usually the 'somebody' that came along was one or both of our then-boyfriends, because Tracy usually told them where we were going.

"Hold Honey for a minute," she handed me the reins. "There's that heron that lets you get real close before it flies off. I'm going to try to get a picture." She had her small camera on her belt, and she was removing it as she moved toward the Coral Cove trail where the heron was stalking an invisible frog.

It happened so fast. I'd turned to rub Honey's velvet nose and when I turned back, Tracy had vanished. I'd heard a kind of "oo" sound so, thinking she might have fallen into the slight declivity that marked the beginning of the trail, I pulled Honey along toward the spot. But I'd only gone about two steps when I saw her trying to come back up to the main path. Someone had her by the arm. She turned to strike at him, and the man—Harley—managed to grab her around the waist. They grappled and fell back down into the hollow.

"Hey!" I shouted, dropping Honey's reins and running full tilt, pulling my can of pepper spray from my jacket pocket.

"Stay back!" yelled Hardwick, pelting past me from the direction we'd come from, down the path to the Cove trailhead. Another man was right behind him, and two more were coming from the other directions.

I kept running. This was my friend, who I had promised to help and who I had led out here to flush a killer. But how had Hardwick known?

Tracy burst into view near the top of the Cove trail, a long scarf trailing from her neck. She pulled it off as she ran out on a finger of land which ended in cliffs. Either she didn't see Hardwick and the others or didn't recognize them as allies. We could hear the waves booming on the rocks as Harley dashed out just fast enough to elude the sheriffs and follow Tracy onto the narrow finger. The four deputies formed a line at the end of the spit where Harley and Tracy were warily circling. I saw that Harley had a bloody nose.

"Good," I thought. Then I noticed that he was crying.

"Why won't you love me, Mary?" he pleaded. "You could be the real Mary. We could be happy, live on the ranch. I'm going to get it all back. Please, Mary. You said you liked the ranch."

"Mary's gone, Harley," Tracy said with amazing gentleness. "She can't live on the ranch, and neither can you. The ranch is gone. We have to move on, Harley. Mary would want us to."

For a moment, bowlegged, droopy-pantsed Harley stood tall. You could see that once he had been a comely young man with a ranch and a future. Then misery and a low cunning slid over his face like a mask. "You just tell me that. You don' know what Mary wants. Mary is dead. I should know. I killed her. There. You happy, Mary? 'Cause I'm goin' to kill you, too."

"Why, Harley?" I couldn't believe Tracy's calm. "We were friends once."

"I don' want no more friends," Harley sneered. "I want me a wife. But Mary said 'no.' All the Marys said 'no'. An' now, you gonna say 'no', too."

Hardwick shook his head almost imperceptibly, but Tracy saw it. Harley saw it, too, and lunged for her, just as she was saying,

"I won't say 'no', Harley. I'd be proud to..." She saw him leap for her, but didn't move until he was close. Too close, I thought. Then she faked left and went right. Harley went for her left, missed her, stumbled, and went over the cliff without a sound. We were all motionless with shock for a few seconds. Then I ran past the deputies to Tracy, while the four men went to the edge of the cliff to peer over.

Hardwick shook his head. "Poor son of a bitch."

The small, wiry brown deputy with a big grin who'd followed Hardwick to the edge said, "Yeah. If he wanted a wife, he coulda had mine." The other deputies winced, but then grinned.

Tracy was still unnaturally calm. "It's OK to have hysterics now, Trace," I said. "But if you're not going to, maybe I will. How come you're so calm? I'm shaking like a leaf and I need to sit down."

I did. I sat right in the dirt and Tracy sat cross-legged beside me and told me that she had felt Mary's presence nearby and Mary somehow, without words, let Tracy know that it would be OK.

Hardwick joined us. "Is that pepper spray legal?" He eyed me fiercely. "How come you two were out here today? Did you know this might happen? Think you could handle it yourself?" His tone conveyed that he definitely didn't think so.

"Yes," I replied. "We were enjoying the gorgeous day. Yes, I thought it might happen. And yes, I thought I could handle it myself and I might have. But we'll never know, will we?"

"You could have lost your friend," he said softly.

Then I started to cry, because he was right. I'd brought Tracy out here on my hunch that maybe Harley was after her, not Melly, confusing Tracy with her aunt from so many years ago. I'd been right, and I'd put her life in danger. I'd been so sure I could handle it—didn't I always? But the moment I looked up and saw that she had vanished was the worst of my life so far.

"Kaia, it's OK." Tracy had her arm around my shoulders and was rocking us slightly. "How long have we been friends? Don't you think I knew what you were up to? But I knew we could handle it. Well, I thought we could. But I'm glad Lt. Hardwick and his men were out here. Why *were* you out here, by the way?"

Hardwick mumbled something.

"What?" we said in unison.

"Jolene told us to come," said the two burly deputies.

"Mary told her," said Tutoy, the wiry one.

* * *

Jolene says Mary is at peace. She doesn't say exactly how she knows, but we believe her. Jax and Melly are thriving, as is Readerss Roost Books. But Mrs. Wanita is watching the front of their house like a hawk day and night and cannot be bought off with even the juiciest paperback romances. Even she never caught the note-dropper. Jax is threatening to sneak over to her house at midnight and paint her windows black.

My Hawai'ian tour went off extremely well, and the addition of Detective Lt. Hardwick and his wife Jolene added a lot, especially when Jolene began to hear from my ancestors in the canyons of Kaua'i. I must admit to some jealousy. Aloha was spoiled rotten by my mother and Uncle Kimo, but she was glad to see me. Almost as glad as I was to see her.

Lt. Hardwick and his men were off-duty the day they followed Tracy and me into Montana de Oro. They turned in an accident report on Harley Boissart, who was buried as he wished on the last piece of land he lived on, far from his mother, Mary. So officially, the murder of Mary Larkton is unsolved, but unofficially, Los Osos is a small town, and the most closely guarded secrets spread the fastest.

Tracy has asked me and Aloha to move in with her at her new apartment, which is large, bright, and faces Shark Inlet, a finger of Morro Bay where hikers, riders, and surfers pass on their way to dunes and waves. It's beautiful. Although I love Kaua'i, I'm considering it, both for business reasons and because the schools in Los Osos are good. It's a good place to raise a child. A place to build memories. And a place where one memory, at last, is laid to rest.

Susan Tuttle

This piece was written in my class. Students (and teacher) chose a slip from the infamous "Peppermint Box," each of which has an opening line on it, and 10 minutes to write. I ended up with the slip that read, "They never knew who the artist was..." and this is what came out in those 10 minutes.

Miracle Painting
by
Susan Tuttle

They never knew who the artist was, there was no signature, but the painting took the world by storm. Someone snapped a photo of it with their iPhone at a small art festival and uploaded it to his Facebook page. It was just his way of showing his friends how he had spent the day with his girlfriend, what he was willing to suffer through for love. But the photo sparked people's imaginations and within hours it went viral.

Everyone saw something different in the brush strokes and swirls of paint: Rainbows; birds flying over the water; the sun sinking into the ocean; elk and deer grazing on diminishing meadowlands. The painting seemed to change depending on the eyes that beheld it; the phenomenon was discussed for months. One person saw a mother clasping her dying child. Another, standing beside that witness, saw two puppies cavorting with a toddler. No one knew how the painting had been created, or what kind of medium was used. Tests were no help; each one identified something different: oils, water color, acrylics.

The Miracle Painting, as it came to be called, changed the world. People began to understand that every one of them created reality, each in their own way. They started to take pains to create more positive realities, realities they wanted to live in and celebrate rather than live through and regret.

And deep within the forest, the artist opened a vein in both body and spirit and began yet another miracle.

Dianne Emley

Dianne Emley is a *Los Angeles Times* and Amazon bestselling author who has received critical acclaim for her Detective Nan Vining mysteries (including *Killing Secrets*), Iris Thorne mysteries (including *Pushover*), and a standalone paranormal thriller, *The Night Visitor*. Her books have been translated into six languages. An L.A. native, she lives in the Central California wine country with her husband, where she's a pretty good cook, an amateur oenophile, and a terrible golfer. About Dianne's books, Tess Gerritsen says: "Emley masterfully twists, turns, and shocks." http://www.dianneemley.com

The idea for "The Last Wife" was sparked a few years ago when I was having dinner out at Café Bizou, a favorite Pasadena restaurant, with two gal pals. I'd lived in Pasadena for years and love to set stories in that beautiful and interesting city. That's where I set my popular Detective Nan Vining mystery series.

That night at dinner with my friends, let's call them Tricia and Jackie, the conversation drifted to the marriage history of Tricia's husband. Let's call him Stan. Tricia and Stan had a long and happy marriage, but I knew that he'd been married before. I asked Tricia, "You're Stan's third wife, right?"

Tricia didn't answer right away and Jackie, who'd known Tricia and Stan longer than I had, helpfully said, "Fourth wife."

I tactlessly blurted, my tongue loosened by chardonnay, "You're Stan's *fourth* wife?"

Tricia turned her pretty brown eyes on me and said, "No, Dianne. I'm Stan's *last* wife." She slowly blinked as an edge of her mouth drew back in a knowing smile.

That phase, "the last wife," stuck in my head. I eventually crafted a story around it.

THE LAST WIFE
by
Dianne Emley

"I told Gary that if he tried to leave me, I'd kill him." Kiki Sumner laughed and took a sip of her martini. "He knows I'd do it, too. I told him that I'm not just his third wife, I'm his *last* wife." She enjoyed being outrageous.

Betts Engleford playfully slapped Kiki's toned arm. Little that came out of Kiki's mouth surprised her anymore. Betts knew that Kiki's larger-than-life persona hid an underlying insecurity. The fiery look on Kiki's face while scrutinizing both their husbands, who were fawning over their comely new associate, Annabelle, convinced Betts that there was at least a glimmer of truth in Kiki's threat.

"Kiki, you know that Gary's completely devoted to you." Betts sipped from her glass of pinot noir.

"He is. Usually. And I love him to the moon and back *but...*" Kiki raised her index finger, displaying a manicured hand festooned with enough gems to skirt being over-the-top. Straddling that fine line had become her brand. "Here's the deal. Gary's worth a lot more to me dead than divorced. If we divorce, I get a tiny settlement according to our prenup, but if Gary dies, his will leaves me well provided for." She let out a throaty laugh. "Looks like a loophole to me."

Betts and Kiki were peering out from behind drapes beside French doors that were opened to the terrace of the Sumners' newly renovated manse off Linda Vista, overlooking the Rose Bowl. Kiki had drawn Betts away from a circle of guests she'd been chatting with to point out Gary and Paul--Betts' husband--standing on the terrace with Annabelle, the two men in thrall as she animatedly recounted some story.

The Sumners were hosting a holiday party for the employees and spouses of Crown City Partners. Paul Engleford and Gary Sumner had founded the once highly regarded Pasadena venture capital firm after earning their MBAs at USC, where they'd met. CCP had hit a rough patch over the past year. The firm had eked out a profit after Paul and Gary had completed a painful downsizing and reorganization, which included bringing in Paul and Betts' son, Matthew. Paul was grooming Matt to take over his role as managing partner. Annabelle Hill had also been brought on with Paul and Gary boasting that her fresh perspective was just what CCP needed. Lacking the stellar job history and top-notch education of CCP's other associates, the pretty twenty-eight-year-old was an unlikely candidate. What she did bring to the table, other than adding a spark of sex appeal to the straight-laced firm, was a deep-pocketed client, her former employer, The Merton Group, run by Carl Merton, whose investments had helped keep CCP afloat over the past year.

Annabelle's hiring out-of-the-blue and without the partners' usual thorough vetting process made Kiki suspicious that there was something else behind the leggy brunette's hearty welcome into the firm. Betts hadn't shared with Kiki, nor would she, that she also found Annabelle's presence at CCP deeply unsettling.

With the setting sun, queen palm trees surrounding the terrace cast long shadows across the travertine. The pleasantly warm daytime temperature grew chilly and women in cocktail dresses began rubbing their bare arms and draping wraps around their shoulders. Waiters lit candles in crackle glass holders on the patio tables and along the deck railings. Inside the house, waiters illuminated tall tapers in candelabras. Still more help circulated with trays of hors d'oeuvres, wine, sparkling water, and took orders for cocktails prepared at the bar inside the house.

Kiki had hired The Kitchen for Exploring Foods to handle the party, not risking engaging anyone other than the go-to caterer favored by Pasadena's savviest hostesses. She'd never felt at ease in her role as an executive's wife and feared making social missteps. Even though she had fun with her flashy persona, it was a front to disguise her self-doubt and perception that she was an outsider in Pasadena's society circles, in spite of her and Gary's wealth. She didn't have Betts' easy confidence as a hostess. Betts amazed Kiki by cooking and serving at her parties herself, bravely trying out recipes for the first time, with only her longtime housekeeper to help clear dishes and Paul manning the bar. But Betts had grown up in a rarified, old money world and, to Kiki, never felt uncomfortable in her skin or that she needed to prove anything to anyone.

"You know what my dear momma from Waco, Texas told me," Kiki began, leaning into Betts. "She said, 'Honey, when a man marries his mistress, he leaves a job opening.'"

Kiki followed up with what she'd guessed Betts was thinking but was too polite to say. "Just so you know, Gary was separated from his second wife before we started dating. I punished him with dead-lifts and drop squats until he made the split official." She'd been Gary's personal trainer and was fifteen years his junior. She tilted her head back and laughed, following with a guilty shrug. "Well, we did have a little hanky panky before that."

Betts smiled cryptically. Her mother, Sarah Ludlow, had taught Betts to listen, ask questions about others, and say little about herself or her own views. Because of that, she was known as a good conversationalist.

Kiki leveled a gaze at the woman her husband was cajoling. "She's not married but I wonder if she has a boyfriend."

"I don't know." Betts glanced at Annabelle.

Gary's booming laughter reverberated all the way inside the house. A former tackle on USC's football team, he had a big personality that matched his size. He'd begun shaving his head when he'd started losing his hair and his bald pate gave him a hipster vibe. He was CCP's salesman.

Paul was the firm's numbers guy and content to be in the background behind colorful Gary. The firm's recent financial downturn, caused by bad investment decisions, was affecting their decades-long friendship. Gary's freewheeling attitude about spending his and the firm's money, which had worsened after he'd married Kiki five years ago, wasn't helping the discord between the business partners.

Betts watched Paul sip his gin and tonic. She enjoyed taking in her husband from a distance, pretending that she hadn't known him for decades and was seeing him for the first time. She admired his tall and lean physique, his upper body sculpted by daily swimming at the Rose Bowl aquatic center or their backyard pool. She'd always loved his wavy, strawberry blond hair. The gray creeping in at the temples added a certain gravitas. Still, he'd never lost his boyish and nerdy side, heightened by his trademark tortoiseshell glasses and hand-tied bow tie.

Betts saw Annabelle move close to say something to Paul, her full lips almost touching his face. Betts had to admit that the young associate was fetching in a figure-hugging sheath in a bold, multi-color print that set off her tan. Her red high heels, bolder than anything Betts would ever wear, flattered her long legs. Her lush hair cascaded over one shoulder. She had a habit of lowering her eyelids with their dark fringe of lashes and letting her full lips part just a bit when she was listening. The whole package was overtly sexual in a way that Betts, schooled in proper behavior at cotillion and by her own strict mother, couldn't pull off if she tried. She had tried and ended up looking as if she were going to a costume party.

Annabelle cracked up at something Paul said, pressing her fingertips against his hand, letting them rest there long enough for the gesture to turn from friendly to seductive. A crooked smile crossed Paul's lips.

Betts knew that smile. "Kiki, take a look at Annabelle flirting with Paul and he's enjoying it, if that makes you feel better."

Kiki made a dismissive noise. "Betts, you can be absolutely certain that *you're* the last wife. You and Paul are a perfect team and you're both still having fun. Matthew and Jessica are great kids—adults, I should say—and doing fantastically. You and Paul make it all look so easy. Lord knows it isn't. You're my hero."

"Thank you." Kiki might have noticed a shadow crossing Betts' bright blue eyes if she hadn't been so caught up in her own drama. Betts said, "Takes a lot of compromise. Knowing when to speak and what to say and when to keep your mouth shut."

"Something I've never mastered." Kiki lustily laughed. "How many years have you two been married?"

"Thirty." At fifty-three years old, Betts was still as trim and attractive as ever but the years spent golfing, horseback riding, and gardening in the California sun had taken a toll on her skin. She wasn't the type to bother with cosmetic dermatology or plastic surgery. She'd learned at her mother's knee that she was not a beautiful woman. Her mother schooled her that prettiness came from inside. People often told Betts that she was one of the nicest individuals they'd ever known. That pleased her.

"This isn't any of my business, but do you and Paul have a prenup?" Kiki asked. "I imagine your parents would have insisted, with your family money and all."

Betts came from old money, the solid kind, from land and transportation, and the quiet kind. The Ludlow family fortune entered the public eye through philanthropic largesse including the Ludlow Pavilion at Huntington Hospital, Ludlow buildings at Caltech, PCC, and USC, and Ludlow scholarships and fellowships.

Betts and Paul lived comfortably but not flashily in a well-maintained, hundred-year-old colonial home in Pasadena's Madison Heights neighborhood. Their biggest luxury was their Lake Tahoe compound, which was perfect for family get-togethers. Paul and Betts' pleasures were simple—spending time with family and friends and watching USC Trojan football from the longtime Ludlow family block of seats.

Betts' patient smile conveyed her answer to Kiki who said, "Right. None of my business. I'm a nosy big-mouth and you're sweet to put up with me. Besides, you and Paul are indestructible."

Betts gazed at her husband and said quietly, "People change."

Kiki didn't hear her friend's cryptic comment because the party planner had stepped from the dining room and signaled to her.

"Time for dinner." Kiki downed the last of her martini, pulled an olive from a toothpick with her teeth, and dropped the toothpick into a potted fern. She began promenading, tapping her big diamond ring against the rim of the crystal glass to sound a chime as she announced, "Dinner is served in the dining room."

Betts beamed when her son Matthew came up and offered his arm. She took it and gave it a squeeze. "Where have you been?"

Matt looked like a younger version of his father. "Talking with Debbie." She was Paul's and Gary's longtime administrative assistant. "Discussing the Carl Merton news."

"What news?"

"Didn't Dad tell you? Merton's being investigated by the SEC for fraud. He's suspected of running a Ponzi scheme."

Normally unflappable Betts gaped at her son. "What does that mean for Crown City Partners?"

"We could be investigated too, for money laundering."

"When did this come out?"

"Last week. I'm surprised Dad didn't tell you. We also found out that Merton's ex-wife took out a restraining order against him. He threatened to shoot her and her boyfriend."

Betts recovered her composure, stoically absorbing the bad news. She watched as Gary walked with Annabelle toward the house, guiding her with his hand on her waist which slipped down to caress one of her butt cheeks. The stolen gesture was brief but Betts saw it and so did Paul who was seething as he walked behind his partner and their new associate. He was focused so intently on Gary and

Annabelle that he didn't notice his wife and son standing just inside the door.

Matt called, "Dad."

Paul turned. "There you are. And there's my bride." He kissed Betts lightly on the cheek. She gave him a frosty smile.

The Crown City Partners offices were on the sixth floor of a building on the corner of Lake and Green in downtown Pasadena. Betts had decorated the suite for the holidays with her usual panache. She encouraged the employees to add personal ornaments to a huge Scotch pine tree in the lobby. Fresh garland and twinkling lights were strung around the nest of cubicles and the office doorways. Tables in the lunchroom were laden with Betts' homemade treats and goodies sent from clients and vendors.

Gary and Matthew were in Paul's office, discussing the Carl Merton problem.

Paul was at his desk, which was adorned with silver-framed photos of his family and pets. On a credenza behind him was a collection of awards and commendations he'd received through the years.

Gary was sitting in one of the two leather guest chairs, drumming his hands against the arms. Matthew leaned against a filing cabinet in a corner by a window.

"We need to separate ourselves from Carl Merton," Gary said. "ASAP. We can't wait until the feds subpoena our books, for crying out loud."

In contrast with Gary's agitation, Paul was calm. "We have nothing to hide."

Gary stood and began pacing. "Our reputation is everything. John Barber and Tyler Williams called me about pulling their money out of CCP because of our involvement with Merton. They've invested about two million. We can take that hit but if more people bail out, especially some of our big guys, we could go belly up."

"Merton plans to go big into TechGen." Paul took off his glasses and rubbed his eyes. "Not having that money will sink their second round of funding."

"We'll find other investors." Gary began cracking his knuckles on the fingers of his left hand as he paced. "I'll break the news to Merton that we're severing our business relationship, today if possible. If he gets ticked off, too bad."

"Make sure he doesn't have a gun with him." Matt peered through a glass panel beside the office door that gave a view of the cubicles where the associates worked. "What about Annabelle Hill? She's been with us for six months and hasn't brought in any clients other than Merton."

"The Merton Group was critical to our survival, Matt." Paul patiently looked at his son. "If Merton hadn't invested with us we'd have had to lay off even more folks."

"Annabelle's a sweet kid." Gary started on the knuckles of his right hand. "She's mortified about this Merton fiasco."

"I don't know how *sweet* she is. What I do know is that she has great legs and a sketchy resume." Matt raised his hand in the direction of the building's garage. "Did you see that new BMW convertible she's driving? That model sells for over a hundred thousand dollars. And she just bought a house. We're not paying her that much. Is Merton giving her kickbacks or is there something else going on between them?"

Paul put his glasses back on. "That's a harsh accusation, Matt." His shoulders relaxed when Gary finished cracking his knuckles, a habit that annoyed Paul. "She could be leasing that car."

Gary paced the room with his big shoulders hunched as he studied the carpet. Minutes passed with no one speaking until Gary said, "I haven't heard about a personal relationship between Annabelle and Merton, but she was his protégé. Our investors need to feel confident that we've cut all ties with Merton. Annabelle's gotta go. Let's give her three months' pay and call it a downsizing." He headed toward the door.

Paul raised a hand. "Hold on. I'm not convinced we need to go to extremes at this point by divesting Merton's money and firing Annabelle too."

Gary turned from the door, frowning at his partner.

"Firing somebody before Christmas is cruel." Paul raised his small, round chin. "Feels a little... I don't know. Vindictive."

Gary glared at Paul. "What are you getting at? Are you suggesting I want to fire Annabelle because of a personal issue with her?"

"I'm just saying that the timing is cruel."

A mirthless smile spread across Gary's lips. "Have you been drinking Kiki's Kool-Aid? I'm *not* having an affair with Annabelle. Sure, I've flirted with her. That doesn't mean anything. I'm a flirt. My sole motive for letting Annabelle go is that I *need* Crown City to survive. I'm not sitting on a mountain of family money and neither are any of our employees. People's livelihoods are at stake."

Matt silently watched the exchange from his corner.

Paul's voice remained measured but a slight tightening at the edges of his eyes betrayed his annoyance at Gary having alluded to the Ludlow fortune. Paul had grown up in an upper middle class family but when he'd married Betts, he'd become rich and it still felt awkward to him. "Of course I want Crown City to thrive, now and into the future. Why else would I bring my son into the firm?" He raised his hands and made a calming motion. "Let's take some time to think things over. We can certainly give it the weekend."

"No later than Monday." Gary left the office.

Once Gary had closed the door, Matt moved toward one of the chairs facing his dad's desk and sat down. He hesitated before speaking.

His father prompted him. "What's on your mind, buddy?"

"Is there something going on that I don't know about? I've never seen you and Gary at each other's throats like this. Even things between you and mom… I feel like something's off lately with everything."

Paul took a deep breath, exhaled, and relaxed into his chair with his hands along the arms. "Business has been tough. Tempers have been running high. Now there's this Merton thing. Your mom… Well, you know Mom. She always gets stressed out during the holidays. Does too much, trying to make everything nice for everyone else." He smiled. "Everything's fine. Everything will be okay."

Matt nodded but didn't seem convinced. "What about Gary and Annabelle? Sounded to me like he was protesting too much about not having an affair with her."

"I've known Gary for a long time and sometimes he doesn't think with the head that's on his neck. But if he says he's not having an affair with Annabelle, I have to take him at his word. He pressed me to hire Annabelle, but I can't lay all the blame on him. I came around and agreed that she'd be an asset to the firm. I didn't work out." He shrugged. "Still, we need to give it the weekend before making a decision that will be damaging to her."

"I admire that about you, Dad. You always put other people first." Matt rose from the chair.

"Are you bringing your girl over for dinner on Sunday?"

"Absolutely. Right now, I'm going to the gym and try to clear my head. See you later."

"You can count on it. Please close the door when you leave. I have a couple of calls to make."

When Paul was alone, he sat back in his chair and stared into space. The strain that he'd tried to keep under control during the meeting returned and threatened to overwhelm him. He felt trapped by forces bigger than he, feelings that were foreign and troubling to him.

Kiki opened one of the big doors of The Derby and was momentarily blinded when she stepped inside the dim restaurant from the bright glare of the hazy December day. She told a hostess, who was standing behind a podium, "I'm just going to have a glass of wine at the bar," unnecessarily adding, "I'm killing time between appointments."

She walked past glass cabinets lining the walls that were crammed with horse racing memorabilia and entered a spacious cocktail lounge. It was quiet as the horses weren't racing today at the nearby Santa Anita Racetrack. Only a few people were at the long bar and the cocktail tables.

Kiki's tight leather jeans and gold-and-silver metallic top attracted the barflies' attention. She climbed onto a stool and looped a lock of blond hair around an ear, showing off a sparkly red earring in the shape of an old-fashioned Christmas tree light. She ordered a glass of champagne from a young, good-looking bartender, flashing a big smile at him.

While the bartender poured Kiki's champagne, she glanced around the room, stopping with surprise when her eyes landed on a discreet corner table where Betts was sitting with a man who Kiki didn't recognize. A waiter came stopped by the table just then, bringing cups of coffee and removing empty plates, presumably from Betts' and the man's lunch. Betts' companion was tall with salt-and-pepper hair and might have been in his fifties. When the waiter left, he and Betts again became engaged in intense conversation, sitting close together.

Wide-eyed, Kiki turned to face the bar, picked up her champagne, and wondered aloud, "What's Betts doing way out here? I've never even heard her mention The Derby." She leaned back and risked another peek at the corner table. Her eyes again widened when Betts' companion picked up her hand and held it between both of his and Betts caressed his cheek with her other hand. For a second, Kiki thought they might kiss, but Betts pulled her hands away and placed them around her coffee cup.

Kiki shook her head. "Never in a million years—"

"Ma'am?" the bartender asked.

"Oh. Nothing. Just talking to myself."

Kiki was debating whether to go over and say hello or to pay for her drink and slip out when Betts and her friend rose to leave.

As Betts approached the bar, she saw Kiki. "Oh, hello. What a surprise."

"Hi, Betts. This *is* a surprise." Kiki slid off the stool and she and Betts hugged. Kiki gave a big, expectant smile to the stranger. Up close, she saw that he was good-looking in a more rugged way than Paul. He was wearing dark slacks and a light blue dress shirt with no tie.

"What brings you out here?" Betts smoothed her hair.

The man said nothing and seemed a little amused as he looked from Kiki to Betts.

"I had my car serviced and I'm waiting for my dressmaker. She's fitting me for a killer dress I'm having made for the Valley Hunt Club's New Year's Eve party."

"I'm sure your dress will be stunning." Betts pulled down the hem of her red-and-green tartan cardigan sweater. "Well... See you soon."

Kiki stepped in front of Betts. "And who did you have lunch with today?"

Betts fumbled for a response, which Kiki knew was quite unlike her. "Oh. Of course. Ah, Forrest Curry, I'd like to present my friend, Mrs. Kiki Sumner."

He extended his hand. "I'm very happy to meet you, Kiki."

"A pleasure. How—"

"I've gotta fly, honey." Betts started walking and said without turning back, "I'll call you."

Forrest gave Kiki a nod and followed Betts.

It was nearly noon on Monday and Annabelle Hill still hadn't shown up for work, even though Paul's assistant Debbie had left a message that he wanted to see her in his office at nine.

Paul peered at a financial statement on his computer monitor but was having a hard time concentrating. Over the weekend, he'd come to the decision that Gary was right and terminating Annabelle's employment was best for the firm.

Gary gave a quick knock on Paul's open door before entering his office.

"You're back." Paul sat back in his chair, happy to take a break from the spreadsheet. "How did it go with Merton?"

"It went, but not well. I met him at the Starbucks in the Paseo. Glad I did it in a public place. Handed him his check. He got back all his money and then some, but he still went off on me, saying that he's not a criminal and ending our relationship with him makes it look like he is. This is revenge... His face turned bright red and he's spitting all over me while he's talking. Everybody's staring. I said, 'Revenge for what?' He says, 'You know exactly what I'm talking about." Gary raised his hands and looked at the ceiling. "I don't. Do you?"

Paul shook his head, blinking. "What did you do?"

"I left. Started walking down Colorado Boulevard and he followed me. Get this... He yelled, 'Did Annabelle put you and that partner of yours up to this? Is she adding insult to injury?'"

The color drained from Paul's face.

Gary continued. "I'd had enough. I pointed at the sawed-off runt and said, 'Carl, this conversation is over. You got your money back. I never want to see you around the Crown City Partners office or bothering any of our employees.' Like the little bully he is, he backed down. Just stood there, red-faced and sweating. I went to my car. Took a moment and then I called our investors who were disturbed by the Merton dust-up and told them we're no longer doing business with The Merton Group. They were happy to hear it."

Paul was silent for a few beats before realizing that Gary had stopped talking. "Definitely."

"What was he talking about—you and Annabelle putting me up to this?"

"No clue. He was just raving, I guess."

"Have you heard from Annabelle?"

Paul shook his head. "I called her house and cell phone. No answer. The termination documents and check for her severance pay are ready. Maybe someone tipped her off about us firing her today."

"I can't imagine who. The only people who know are you, me, Matthew, and Debbie and she's kept bigger secrets than this."

"I just hope that Annabelle's okay. It's strange for her to not answer her cell phone."

Gary watched as Paul ran his fingers back and forth across the carved edge of his desk while staring at the surface, looking disturbed. "No big deal, Paul. If Annabelle won't come into the office, get Debby to send her a certified letter with her check. Have the suite's key cards reprogrammed and notify building security not to let in either her or Merton. Good riddance to both of them."

Paul continued to stare a hole into his desk.

Gary clapped his hands. "How about some lunch?"

Breaking his trance, Paul pushed up from his chair. "Sounds great."

They walked out of the building to the street and headed toward Smitty's on the opposite side of Lake. While standing with a group of people who were also waiting for the light to change, Gary muttered, "Uh oh."

Paul turned to see what had drawn Gary's attention and saw Carl Merton rapidly walking toward them.

"Let's go." Gary grabbed Paul's arm and started pulling him back toward the office building.

The streetlight changed and people began crossing the street. Merton started to jog after Gary and Paul, pulling a pistol from his jacket pocket and aiming it at them.

A woman shouted, "He's got a gun!"

People yelled and scrambled for cover. Car tires screeched and horns blared.

Pushing people aside, Gary, dragging Paul behind him, had nearly reached the glass doors into the building. A bullet hit the window of a ground floor yoga salon, scattering the people taking a class there. Merton kept shooting, aiming wildly. Gary opened a door into the lobby, having lost his grip on Paul, threw himself onto the ground and shimmied for cover behind furniture.

He peeked from behind a couch to see Paul on the sidewalk outside the door. He was bleeding but Gary couldn't see where Paul had been shot. Merton walked up to Paul, aiming his gun at him. Paul put up his hands and shrank away from Merton but there was nowhere to go. It tortured Gary to hear Paul pleading for his life.

Gary watched in horror as Merton bared his teeth and spewed words at Paul that Gary couldn't make out. He bolted up and shouted to distract Merton, but it was hopeless. Merton fired his gun at Paul, who crumpled into a ball, jolting with each bullet. Merton kept shooting until his gun was empty.

Merton stood over Paul's bloody body and seemed almost calm, holding the gun by his side. Motion inside the lobby drew his attention and he looked to see Gary ducking behind a couch. Merton raised his empty gun at him in a perverse wave before beginning to walk down the now empty sidewalk, the gun dangling from his hand.

Police cars sped to the scene with lights and sirens. Cops with guns drawn, using their cars for cover, shouted at Merton to throw down his weapon and drop to the ground. After a moment's hesitation, he complied. He was quickly pushed face-down against the pavement and handcuffed.

Gary returned to his fallen friend and was surprised to find him still alive. Paul tried to speak. Trembling, Gary said, "Stay quiet."

Paul managed to crook his bloody fingers, signaling Gary to draw near. He did and heard Paul say, right before he died, "Tell Betts I'm sorry."

Betts had already heard about the shooting in downtown Pasadena by the time Matthew had arrived at the house. When he tearfully told his mom that Dad was dead, she collapsed.

Police found Annabelle Hill on the floor of her bedroom of her Bungalow Heaven cottage, dead from gunshot wounds. Scattered around her body were photographs of Annabelle and Paul in compromising and shocking positions.

A year later, Betts and her children honored the first anniversary of Paul's murder by visiting his grave and later having dinner together at the Parkway Grill, Paul's favorite restaurant. The following week, Betts treated herself to lunch at the Langham Hotel's poolside café. It was a mild December afternoon. Visitors there savored the California winter sun and so did the locals, who never tired of it.

Betts poured more Darjeeling tea from a small porcelain pot into her cup.

It had taken months and the help of a psychotherapist for Betts to stop blaming herself for Paul and Annabelle's murders. She'd finally accepted that, regardless of her role in the circumstances that had led to the tragic events, Carl Merton was the one who had pulled the trigger.

She also stopped regretting having asked her old college buddy, Forrest Curry, who was now a private investigator, to look into her suspicions that Paul, who had uncharacteristically started taking long lunches and not coming home right after work, was having an affair.

She'd expected her and Paul's marriage to change after Matthew and Jessica were on their own and had moved out for good. Steadfast Paul had never before strayed. He'd never even engaged in a serious flirtation. As for Betts, an affair wasn't in her vernacular. Still, when her radar detected that Paul might be up to something, she wasn't completely surprised and wrote the fling with Annabelle off to a mid-life crisis. Still, it had to end.

When she'd confronted Paul with the sordid photographs that Forrest's associates had taken, Paul had given Beth the shock of her life."I want a divorce," he'd told her. "Annabelle and I are getting married."

Stunned and hurt by Paul's revelation, Betts had told Paul what Forrest had found out about his paramour. "Annabelle and Carl Merton are sleeping together. She threw herself at you only because she wanted to use you as a patsy to bring Merton and his dirty money into Crown City Partners."

Paul had again shocked her. "I know. That's how things started between Annabelle and me, but then we fell in love."

"*Love?* Are you out of your mind? You really think she *loves* you?" Betts had had to sit down. Her head had been spinning.

She had long taken care of life's details, creating a peaceful and happy home for her husband and children, setting up a barrier around them so they could flourish. When anything threatened to tarnish the family, she took care of that, too. She'd become adept at covering Paul's business and personal gaffes. He could be hopelessly naïve. His affair with Annabelle had put everything at stake—their marriage, the business, and the family name. Who knew how it would end up? But for the first time in many years, Betts couldn't do what she knew in her heart needed to be done. She didn't have the guts to take the next step.

"Hello, there." Forrest Curry pulled out a chair at Betts' table and sat down.

"Good afternoon." After a pause, Betts spontaneously gave him a long kiss on the lips. It drew the attention of people nearby but for once, Betts didn't care if she looked unseemly.

Ending the kiss, Betts giggled and touched her smeared lipstick.

"Wow," Forrest said. "I've waited a long time for that."

"It's been a year and a week since Paul's murder."

He picked up her hand and kissed her palm. "An acceptable mourning period. But I'm talking about the thirty years I've waited for you since your mother made you break up with me in college."

"Ah, yes. Mother. She insisted that I marry Paul."

"I wasn't suitable marriage material for Sarah Ludlow's daughter." Forrest's dark eyes sparkled. "She's not going to be happy to hear that you're again cavorting with... What did she call me, 'that rascal'?"

Betts knew her mother had been right back then. Paul was better marriage material than adventurous Forrest. Her union with Paul had been stable, respectable, and productive if not exciting. When Paul wouldn't listen to reason and end his relationship with Annabelle, Betts had turned to her eighty-two-year-old mother for advice.

"Actions have consequences," Sarah Ludlow had reminded her. She'd asked Betts for the damning photos of Paul and Annabelle. When the police had asked Mrs. Ludlow how the photos had ended up in Carl Merton's mailbox, she'd pulled herself erect and told them she did what she had to do.

Betts' friend Kiki liked to joke about being the last wife, but for Kiki, that honor was all about money. Maybe because Betts had always had money, it had never been a source of motivation for her. For Betts, it was a question of honor, legacy, and doing the right thing for the family. She was Sarah Ludlow's daughter, after all, but it had taken her mother, a last wife, to ensure that Betts followed in her footsteps.

"Mother's already guessed about you and me," Betts said.

"And?"

"She says it's a good time for a rascal in my life."

"Glad to know she likes a happy ending."

"She does." Betts added with a wink. "And a rock-solid prenup."

JoAnne Lucas

JoAnne Lucas is a member of both the Central Coast and the San Joaquin chapter of Sisters in Crime. She is also a member of Mystery Writers of America and Private Eye Writers of America. Lately she's been writing her stories for Darkhouse Books' and Untreed Reads' anthologies.

"Retribution Run" was born from the need to write an entry for the San Joaquin Chapter's annual *Coveted Dead Bird Event. The theme that year was Killing The Classics. It took the humor award

*Coveted Dead Bird Event is a short story event. Winner receives a trophy with a stuffed black bird on top, claws up.

How did a nice guy from the farm get mixed up in a power fight between the Musketeers and Cardinal Richelieu's men? Man, that is so 1625!

RETRIBUTION RUN

By

JoAnne Lucas

Friday night, June, 26, 1998
Morro Bay, CA

"Oh, sh—!" Dart swore under his breath when he wiped out on his motorcycle and nearly took three large guys with him. Good thing he was just coasting. The drive-in was a known biker hangout and he'd just lost any chance of impressing those three with his moves.

"You! Toad! You looking to get your body parts donated?" A heavily built rider decked out in tats, jeans and leather chaps dismounted from his bike and leaned over him.

Another guy, tall with an expensive bleached streak job like a model's came up and stood behind the biker. "Yo, *Jefe*, that's too young for a toad. More like a tadpole. Whadda you think, Trey?" he called to the rider further back.

Still on his Harley, the last guy waved it off. "Whatever."

"You didn't answer me, toad. Whatcha' doing here?"

Okay, Dart told himself, *not feeling the love here, guys.* Definitely time to show some macho genes. He tried for a cool dismount from the downed bike, but his stiff new leathers weren't giving him a break and the motorcycle almost took him flat—again. He left the bike on the ground and stood up.

"Er, um—you're the Musk's crew, right?" He nodded at their vest patches—three drawn sabers in the all-for-one position. What he got back was stony stares and silence.

Dart started sweating. "Uh, I've been told you're the guys to go to when you need something back from the Renaissance Cardinals, and I—well, here I am."

"The Cards don't give up what they got," the first biker said. "Go on home, toad, and breathe a little longer."

"But, but they said you could do it. You could help her escape, be safe. And my name's not toad. It's Dart."

"What?" tall-and-blonde asked. "Is that like short for d'Artagnan or sumpthin? Don't believe it. Who calls you that?"

"My grandfather," he mumbled.

"He think you're some kind of swordsman or super hero?"

"No. It's short for Damned Upstart. Gave it to me when I was a kid. I love Grandpa and I won't take any guff from you over my name."

"Whoa there, little tadpole," the tall one said and raised his hands in a peace-making gesture. "I had a grandfather once. Dart it is. We're the Musketeers. I'm Deuce, because I'm so big and twice the fighter of anyone around. This guy here is our leader, *El Jefe*, you know—the chief, the big *Kahuna*. That's Trey over there. He's a triple threat with motorcycles, builds them, races, and can damn near cook dinner while riding on them."

"Nice to meet you," Dart said and inwardly winced. He'd come off sounding like a mama's boy. But—*these* were supposed to be the good guys, the Musketeers, for God's sake. Whatever happened to brotherhood, camaraderie, and true-to-the-end buddies?

El Jefe ran a hand over his shaved scalp. "You got balls, toad, er—Dart. I'll give you that. Okay, not promising anything here, but tell us about your prob."

Dart breathed a little easier and told them about how he met the most wonderful girl in the world and that Rich Lu, leader of the Cardinals and the biggest s.o.b. on wheels, must have frightened or threatened her to make her stay with them. While he's telling them his story he's checking out their Harleys. *Jefe's* was a Fat Boy and had a large red number one painted on the tank. It really stood out against the gray body. Trey had the best silver streams he'd ever seen, and Deuce's sported a pair of wild cards. *Maybe I'll get a sword painted on mine*, he thought. *A rapier or a saber. Yeah!*

El Jefe grunted and looked around. "Hmmm, there's nuthin' doin' here tonight, and I don't like what I'm hearing. It won't hurt to go by Happy Jack's and check on the Cards." He remounted and throttled the Harley, then wheelied his way out of the parking lot. Deuce followed with a rebel yell and neatly cut off a pickup turning in.

Trey started his bike. "You'd better get moving, Dart, or it'll all be over before you get there."

I can only hope. "I'll be right along," he said and waited until the last biker was out of sight before he wrestled his machine upright. Then he rode cautiously out of the parking lot, before he revved it up a little.

Even over the motorcycle's roar he could hear Happy Jack's Bar before he saw it. Square in your face with no apologies, Happy Jack's was home to hardcore drinkers and loud music. The Musks were waiting for him outside. He glided into the parking lot—*Thank you, God!*—and cut the engine.

The bar's door swung open and nine bikers filed out. Each wore black jeans and chaps, with a black leather vest over a long sleeved, red silk shirt. Wicked-looking knives in stiff new sheaths were strapped at their sides. Dart didn't need to check out the crimson vest patch with its fleur-de-lis. The Renaissance Cardinals. The hardest club to ride with, the meanest group to run afoul of. He glanced at the relaxed posture of the three Musks and noted their knives in leather sheaths worn from use. He felt a little confidence surge against his trepidation, but he also felt naked without a knife of his own.

"You! Get that out of here now!"

Was he talking to me? . . . About what?

Trey leaned over and said, "Green bikes are considered bad luck by some in these parts, and Rich Lu is big on superstitions."

"Hmmm." He checked out Rich Lu before he did anything with his bike. Tall, lean and sure in his power, the leader of the Cardinals with his slicked back black hair and trim Fu-Manchu beard looked like the personification of evil. Very effective. Dart put on his casual act as he pushed the green motorcycle around the corner and out of sight. While he shoved the heavy bike he chewed over the situation. Nine against three—no four. Still not nice odds. He'd do anything for Dee, but maybe this confrontation wasn't such a good idea.

When he returned he listened to *Jefe* and the Rich guy negotiate a meet. Rich Lu drew slowly and deliberately on his thin cigarillo. "Tell me, what is at stake for this person?" He blew a disdainful load of smoke at Dart.

Bastard!

Jefe never took his eyes off Rich Lu but snapped his fingers at Dart. Dart blurted, "Deanna Wynter—Dee Wynter."

Complete silence.

"Someone call my name?" A sultry blonde dressed in Card's colors right down to her sturdy riding boots, struck a sexy pose briefly in the doorway then strolled over to Rich Lu. Dart stared at the femme fatale.

That's not my Dee Winter. How could she have changed so fast? What happened to her sweetness, her innocence?

Jefè whirled around and grabbed Dart by the upper arms. "You mean you want us to war over that piece of female? Her? She's not worth it."

Dart shook loose of *Jefè's* hold and threw another look at Dee, holding on to his dream. "I respect you, man, but don't you tell me that. That's my lady. She's special to me. She's mine."

"She never was yours, kid. She's just playing you."

"No, you're wrong. You don't understand. She's my girl."

El Jefè got up into Dart's face. "No, *you* don't understand. She never was your girl. She's. My. Wife." He punctuated every word with a hard jab to Dart's chest. "Not. Your. Girl. Just road trash and not worth fighting over. You feel me on this? *Dart!* I said, we clear on this?"

"Your wife." Dart wanted to cry. A sham. It had all been just a sham with her.

"You looking to back down again, *Jefè*?" Rich Lu drawled. "You wouldn't go up against me for her before. You never could." He tossed the cigarillo. "And so we all know how your pride is burning," he said softly.

"Damn you, my pride is just fine. She's not worth spit. Dart here has been injured by one of yours. I challenge you to an extermination run.

Unrest and whispers waved through the parking lot. Every eye hung tight on *Jefè* and Rich Lu, but Dart looked away after a moment. He couldn't care less about their absurd posturing, he just wanted to go back an hour, a day maybe. To a time when he still believed.

Rich Lu raked Dart with narrowed eyes. "You do this to him?" he asked Dee.

She shrugged. "I was bored."

The leader nodded once and told *Jefe*, "You are right. The young man has been injured and his honor calls for trial by combat." Rich mounted his motorcycle. "We ride to Dead Man's Turnout—now!" He turned and pointed at Dart, "You leave your bike here." Dart watched Dee climb on the back of Rich's bike and snuggle her arms around the Card's waist.

How could she be married to *El Jefe*, have something going on with Rich Lu, and still come on to him? *Jefe* was right, she really wasn't worth risking anything for.

Rich Lu and his men moved out. *Jefe* roared out next, followed by Deuce and a loud   "All for one, and one for all—Yee-haw!" Trey fired up his bike and told Dart to climb on.

"Wait, what's an extermination run?"

Trey throttled back. "Let's just say that by the end of it either the Cards or the Musks will cease to exist." He started to rev his engine.

"No," Dart laid his hand on Trey's arm. "They cease to exist how?"

Trey sighed. "Because they have nine riders against our three, the two leaders will go at it alone. They'll charge at each other until one is unseated. Like a joust."

"A chicken run, you mean."

"Well, yeah. The loser's group must wear their patch upside down with the winner's patch above it. This shows the world that they were beaten by the winners."

"And? What is it you're not telling me?"

Trey looked off in a distance. "Jousting is against the law. Got a lot of deputies out there keeping their eyes peeled for a meet just like this. Add to it that if the Musks lose, we're no longer a crew. We're too shamed. Same thing on the Cards if they lose. Trouble is those boys aren't going to want to play nice afterwards either way. Some heads are likely to get smashed." He looked over at Dart. "You up to that?"

Dart took a turn at distance staring. Head smashing was serious fighting. Nothing like the scrambling he and his cousins used to do back at the ranch. And what about those knives? Good Lord, what had he gotten into?

He mentally shook his head. "What did Rich Lu mean that Dee Wynter had messed with my honor? She wouldn't be the first woman in the world to make a guy think she liked him."

"No, she wouldn't. Met a few of them myself. Thing is —well, Dart, you have two kinds of riders on opposite ends of this arc. You got your outlaws in crews or clubs over here, and your weekenders, guys who go for Sunday rides in groups, over there. Dee talked you into getting and wearing everything that labels you a plastic warrior, the saddest of the sad. Real bikers don't go clanking around with chains hanging halfway to their knees from both their wallets and their hunks of keys. They ruin your paint by banging against the bike and it's too easy for someone to grab hold of and pull you off. Then, no one rides in tight leather pants outside of the movies. You need to be able to move easily after a ride. Wear chaps for protection, jeans for comfort. And that green bike? She set you up for that, too?"

"Yeah."

"Well, there you have it. She damaged you and we're going to make it right. You tight with that?"

Dart nodded, he couldn't trust his voice. He'd lost a dream but gained some heroes, got a load of humiliation and a little respect. He'd figure the score later if he lived long enough. Right now he had to figure what to hold on to as he climbed on Trey's bike.

* * *

The turnout was five miles down from the Cold Spring Tavern and the top of San Marcos Pass. Ninety-some minutes of hard riding through the sweeping curves and twisted switchbacks brought home the lesson about tight pants. Dart couldn't dismount without Trey's arm. He walked in small circles, shaking out his legs to get the circulation moving again. He'd figured that neither Rich nor *Jefè* would back down from the meet, whether he wanted them to or not. This was never about him, he was just the catalyst. He staggered and caught Dee's smirk. It strengthened his resolve to stand by the Musks and take whatever was coming. He'd not be the plastic warrior Dee took him for.

Then he scoped out the area. Three sides of the turnoff dropped away and had only token low barriers to mark the danger zone. With no street or city lights around to blaze away the inky darkness, the Cards had parked their bikes and left their bright beams on along one side of the grade drop off while the riders stood in a loose semi-circle around where the action would take place. Those Cards, Dart thought, with their fancy shirts and black uniforms looked pansy next to his three guys in their cut-off sleeveless shirts and unmatched clothes. That is until he got a good look into their faces. Yeah, those faces were going to haunt his sleep for a time.

Next he checked out the Musks' locations. Trey and Deuce sat on their bikes opposite the Cards, lights on, motors idling. *Jefè* was conferring with Rich Lu in the middle of the ring. He watched as they parted and returned to their men.

Jefè said to Dart, "You get to be my fender ornament, kid. Rich feels you and Dee need to be a part of this. Just remember, she's no lady and she's meaner than a snake. Hold on to that sissy bar and don't make me lose our balance. You get scared and have to pee, I don't want to hear about it. Piss or not, but don't come off my bike. We clear?"

Dart cleared his throat twice. "Yes." He looked back at Trey with his shoulders slouched, arms dangling over the handle bar of his Harley and at Deuce jazzed up and shouting encouragement. He took off his chains and gave Trey his wallet and keys. Trey nodded and clapped him on his shoulder.

"Climb on, kid," *Jefè* called. "We ride!"

Jefè raced the bike into Rich's path. Both bikers dodged and wove perilously close to each other. *Jefè* slowed to make a one-eighty turn and revved up to return. During the second pass Dart felt a massive blow to his right thigh that surprised him and made him loosen his hold on the bar. Dee was looking back over her shoulder at him and laughing. The cheers and whistles from the Cards was unreal.

"Another thing about Dee, kid," *Jefè* shouted at him, "she don't play fair."

No kidding.

"What can I do? I can't kick her back."

"Your choice, but if she gets in a good one and you fall off, we lose. And I don't intend to lose, ever.

Me, neither. He gripped the bike harder and hunkered down.

The next pass Dart timed Dee's kick, blocked it with his boot, and pushed back. She almost lost her balance. Rich's bike wobbled.

"Good one, kid," *Jefè* shouted.

By the fourth run dust hung heavy in the air. Dart saw Dee lean deeply to one side and figured she was going for a high strike to his body or face. He shifted like he was going to block a low kick again, but gripped the bike with his thighs. *Just like riding a horse bareback,* he thought. As her high kick came, he grabbed Dee's ankle with both hands and shoved her off the cycle. Over his shoulder he watched as the Cardinal leader tried to over-compensate for balance and lose control. Rich Lu went down, scruffing up dirt with his pretty red silk shirt.

Dart gave an enthusiastic arm pump. "Yeah!"

The Cardinal leader screamed, "It's all because of that damned green bike."

Jefè hollered, "Slide off now, kid. Quick!"

Dart heard Deuce's rebel yell and the familiar "All for one and one for all!" Both Deuce and *Jefè* barreled straight for the line of Card bikes. They kicked most of the machines into the gorge before roaring out of the turnout. Dart jumped on the back of Trey's bike and knocked over the last of the bikes while Trey dodged an angry knife-wielding biker. Then they ran over Rich Lu's downed cycle and sent the Card's leader scrambling out of their way. Trey circled around and raised his Harley up in a long wheelie in the Cards' faces like a triumphant stallion pawing the air before they took off for the tavern up the hill. Halfway there they pulled up short at the sight of the other two Musks on the side of the road in a tangle of wheels and steel.

El Jefè limped over to them. "Keep going. Deuce wiped out and I ran into him. Busted my wheel base. When you can, call a tow for us. Now, get out of here before the cops or the Cards catch you.

"We'll be at Cold Springs," Trey said.

"You done good, kid." *Jefè* shook Dart's hand. "Honor riding with you."

*   *   *

The crowd at Cold Spring was celebrating. They had sent a rider to scout out the situation at the jousting area. He reported back that Rich Lu had left his bikeless men and Dee behind and evidently took off for the coast. Dee was trying to boss the Cards and that wasn't going over well. The scout left there and on his way back to the tavern passed the first arriving sheriff's car.

So it was drinks all around as several tow trucks, Highway Patrol and more sheriff cars paraded their way down to Dead Man's Turnout over the next hour. The passing of each elicited a toast and jeers from the spectators in the bar.

Nursing a beer and his bruised thigh, Dart asked Trey what he planned to do.

"I'll probably be working on *Jefè*'s and Deuce's bikes at the shop for a couple of weeks. Don't know if *Jefè*'s can be saved this time. Neither will be riding for a while so I guess I'll go my own way."

"You mean you'll leave them? Break up the crew? How can you do that?"

"Whoever heard of the one and a half Musketeers? Hey, you gotta learn to ride with the inner you—not take yourself so seriously. That was Rich Lu's big weakness. He believed all his own mystic stuff. You think *Jefè* and Deuce are sorry 'bout what went down? Hell, no. They're probably remembering—laughing and shaking their heads right now, saying it was a righteous run.

"As for me," Trey pulled the black sweat bandana from his forehead down over the top half of his face. Two holes had already been cut for his eyes. "I'm going to be the Lone Ranger."

Dart smiled and shook his head.

"See," Trey said, "there you go. First time I've seen you smile. Looks good on you." He took a last swig of beer and wiped his mouth. "So, how do you feel about the run? Did it do the job for you?"

Did it? It didn't help with the hurt or shame Dee caused—the way she shredded his beliefs for target practice. But he felt he had somehow been forged by fire and combat into a new shape, a stronger form. One he still needed to get used to, maybe grow into. But, did it do the job for him? Dart nodded once.

"It'll do."

"Good man." Trey stood and hoisted his saddlebag. "You know, we all made history tonight by taking out the Cards. We're the newest legend going. You're pretty handy in a dustup, Dart. Tell you what, you can tag along with me as Tonto."

Dart had an immediate mental picture of his bike painted like a pinto pony. Long way from the saber that he wanted. "No way, Kemo Sabe. I'm looking for more action than offering a few grunts while you call all the shots. Think I'll turn in my bike for a Harley and maybe ask if you guys would, you know, teach me how to really ride." He stood up slowly on his aching legs and shook Trey's hand. "Whatever happens, thanks for all your help tonight, I wouldn't have made it through alive without you."

"No prob and I'll be happy to help you with your ride. My man Charlie over there will give you a lift back to Happy Jack's in his car when you're ready."

A car ride? Thank you, God.

"Thanks, again," he said to Trey.

"Take care of yourself, and, oh yeah—here." Trey handed Dart his wallet, keys and chains from his pack. "And this is for you."

"A lite beer? What's with that?"

"Little remembrance from me to you. See you around."

A deputy came in and announced he wanted to talk with everyone who had bikes out front. Trey slipped out a side door. Dart heard the Harley start up.

"Hey, you," the deputy yelled out the opened doorway, "come back here. I want to talk— Damn it, who was that masked rider?"

Dart grinned, he knew a cue when he heard one. He limped over and handed the deputy the can of Coors Lite Silver Bullet and said, "Wait for it."

"Huh?"

From out of the night, over the roar of a mighty Harley came the cry.

"Heigh-ho Silver, awaaaay!"

Susan Tuttle

I wrote this story for the San Luis Obispo (SLO) NightWriters contest, which had a theme of *deja vu*. When I heard that theme, the opening line popped into my head, and it tickled my funny bone. The story just grew from there. Imagine my disappointment when I discovered that board members were not eligible to enter the contest (I'm the Treasurer and the Newsletter Editor). So I present it here, for you to enjoy.

Not Again

by
Susan Tuttle

I stood in the dark alley with a dead gun in my hand and a smoking body at my feet. *What the hell?* Faint white wisps rose from the bloody holes. Was this real? And who had the guy been talking to? Not me. I glanced around; we were definitely alone. I lifted the gun and stared at it. A feeling of familiarity shivered down my spine and I reached out. It felt as though I pushed through molasses. Or maybe softened glass. Then sirens sounded in the distance, drawing closer, and the moment shattered. Tires squealed nearby. Cops. Time to get the hell out of there.

Jerzy, my partner in crime, waited for me at the mill.

"Things go okay?" she asked.

"Yeah." I unscrewed the gun's barrel and threw it in the smelter. Jerzy frowned at my tone. She knew my moods so well.

"Except?"

I screwed a new barrel onto the gun. No way the cops could trace any bullets to me now.

"He said something weird, just as I shot him."

"What?" Jerzy turned and leaned her bony body against a counter. Inky shadows danced around the huge room.

"He said, 'No, please. Not again.' And he was looking to my left, like someone was standing there, someone only he could see."

"That is weird. Wonder what he meant? It's not like you can kill someone more than once, you know?" Jerzy gave me her come-hither smirk. "Feel free to do me again, though." She air quoted the 'do me.'

"Yeah," I waved a hand, still distracted by the scene in the alley. "The body smoked," I added.

"A cigarette?" Jerzy gave me a sidelong glance, like she feared for my mind. Hell, I'd begun to fear for it, myself. My disdainful snort didn't quite work.

"Give me a break. No, the wounds. A white mist rose from them. Never saw that before." I'd be damned if I'd admit it had felt familiar to me.

Jerzy poured Scotch neat. It sloshed onto the table. She lit a cigarette and lifted her glass. The cancer stick protruded from her fingers like a fragile handle. The lamp behind her limned her profile as she took a sip and threw her head back to savor the smoky burn of the alcohol. A bead of Scotch dropped from the bottom of the glass onto her blouse. Willies shuddered down my spine as the moment slowed and stretched out.

I've lived this before.

The thought wormed its way into my head though I knew it wasn't true. Jerzy had only started smoking the day before I'd left on this last assignment. There was no way her holding both cigarette and glass in the same hand could seem familiar. But it did. Something inside me slipped. The room closed in and my head spun.

"I need some air," I said, rising and stepping out onto the balcony. I lit a cigarette of my own and leaned my elbows on the railing as I studied the Pacific rolling onto Morro Bay's shore.

Man, my deja's are really vu-ing, I thought. It gave me the creeps. I'd done this how many times now, taken out an assigned target? Then come back to Jerzy and her willing body. Too often to count. Not that I really liked the work, it was just okay. But it was easy. And I was damn good at it. Seemed to come natural to me. I tried to eliminate only those who deserved it, though if the money was good enough I didn't bother checking too hard. I like my creature comforts, but working hard to get them doesn't interest me.

Never had bullet holes smoke before, though. Guns, yeah, but not bullet holes. Felt this deja vu thing every once in a great while, too, but never so much in one day. Or quite so clear. Another shiver crawled up my spine. *Shit,* I thought. *Maybe I'm just getting old. Maybe it's time to get out of the business.*

A week later another envelope arrived, one with a payment amount I simply couldn't turn down. It would put my bank balance over into retirement territory. I unfolded the paper that accompanied the bank transfer. Another done-this-before feeling before I even read the name. I almost quit then, but when I saw who it was, I couldn't help but smile. This guy was major scum. Yes, it was a rival syndicate who wanted him eliminated, one even worse than he was, but I'd be doing the world a favor by getting rid of this douche bag.

I arrived early at the location noted on the paper—which I'd burned, as usual—and found a dark spot in the alley where I could wait, unseen, for the creep to show. Four hours later I knew it was a bust. No sign of the target. What had gone wrong? I sure as hell didn't want to return all that money.

I left my hiding place and again that deja vu thing shuddered into me. My heart jerked in my chest. A scrape spun me around. He stood there backlit by the streetlight at the end of the alley, a SIG Sauer pointed at my chest. A chill went through me; I'd been set up.

I went for my gun though I knew it was useless. He popped off two muted shots. They hit me and lifted me off my feet. I stared up at him from the ground. A light shimmered beside him and suddenly a woman stood there, shining and translucent. Tears brimmed in her eyes. Faint traces of white mist rose from the holes in my body.

"What?" I asked her. The gunman looked around, frowned and shook his head. It was obvious he couldn't see her.

"This is your fourth time around," she said. "Yet you refuse to learn, you just keep doing it all wrong. I'm sorry. You have to start over."

"No, please," I said. "Not again."

She just sighed and vanished, and I rode the white mist into yet another new beginning.

Victoria Heckman

Victoria Heckman's first *Hawai'i mystery series* features officer Katrina Ogden, K.O., of the Honolulu Police Department. Her second series, *Coconut Man mysteries of Ancient Hawai'i* begins with *Kapu-Sacred*. Her third mystery series (*Burn Out & Wet Work*) starring animal communicator Elizabeth Murphy is set on California's Central Coast. Stand alone mystery, *Pearl Harbor Blues*, begins on Dec. 7, 1941 and uncovers a dynasty of corporate intrigue. *K.O.'d at Banzai Pipeline* sends her to the big surf contests of O'ahu's North Shore (Jan.2016) She is a member of Sisters in Crime-Central Coast Chapter. Visit her website www.victoriaheckman.com or find her on Facebook,Twitter & Instagram.

I wrote this story after viewing some crime scene photos (long story) and I wondered 'what if you saw yourself in an official crime scene?' Yes, it creeped me out too, but it started this line of thought. I have always liked paranormal stories and loved paranormal mysteries, I'd just never written one. I also love history and thought this was a fun way to 'experience' it. If someone could touch a place and 'go' there, in another time, how fun is that? The apartment building is real, in Hollywood, and really has its own ghost!

Transformation
by
Victoria Heckman

No one wants to see a crime scene. No one wants to *be* a crime scene. Especially a homicide. And I found out the hard way—in a crime scene evidence photo. I saw my own body lying on the floor of the bodega, chips packages and candy bars scattered in the pool of blood under my head.

The last thing I remember was stopping at the convenience store for chips and a diet soda. Although my apartment is on Yucca, way up in Hollywood, I like to play tourist on the weekends when I'm not working.

I teach first grade at a private school up on Mulholland. Well, I did.

Los Angeles is so culturally eclectic that I can find anything I have a craving for in the diverse neighborhoods. That day I was driving around admiring the graffiti. Maybe that sounds weird, but a lot of it is lovely, powerful art—not just "tagging." I got hungry and stopped at a bodega. Just my luck to be rummaging for limon chips, which are actually lime flavored and delicious, when two bangers pushed in and tried to hold up the clerk. I had just dropped my wallet and bent to pick it up and so missed their entrance. They also missed me until I stood and knocked a row of pork rinds off the shelf. The first guy, already jumpy, turned and fired, hitting me in the head.

When I saw the photos later I was splayed amid a pile of pork rinds, one leg bent under me and no wallet. Not a glamorous pose. Turns out after shooting me, then the clerk, they emptied the till and stole my wallet. Joke's on them. I had almost no cash and kept my debit and credit cards in a separate case which I'd left in my purse in the car. All they got was my snack money.

Anyway, the arriving cops checked me but thought I was dead. They started processing the scene and the ambulance crew showed up to take my body to the medical examiner. Thank goodness they decided I was worth attempting to resuscitate because I'd been gone several minutes by then. I don't know how long exactly, but enough to cause me to be unable to return to work and for my problem to show up.

The nurse in the hospital woke me. "Margaret? Ms. Addison? There's a detective waiting for you."

That detective explained what happened and showed me my own crime scene photos. I don't recommend visual aids when learning that you were dead. He was there to see if I could I.D. either of the robbers. Nope. Between me squatting to retrieve my wallet, hitting the pork rinds and dying, I didn't catch much. Grainy surveillance footage on his laptop showed two guys in hoodies burst in (they could have been anyone or even chimps, you couldn't tell) and I saw myself get shot. Then they turned and shot the clerk. I didn't have any emotion attached to it. I thought I would. It wasn't like the movies. It happened so fast. No witty dialog or moment of indecision. I just dropped like a puppet with the strings cut, then the clerk dropped out of view behind the counter. Maybe it helped that it was in black and white. Two cameras, one at each end of the store covered the action, video only, no audio. My spreading blood pool was black and no close up showed either my or the clerk's features. The video was definitely worse than seeing the still photos. The blood was the only moving thing in the shot for minutes until the police arrived. Creepy.

I did get close ups from the crime scene photos. I sure looked dead to me, too. Apparently the bullet grazed my skull not permanently damaging the brain but definitely causing it some problems, which is why I can't work. I now have a nice furrow in my head that will not grow hair, I was informed, my head being bandaged so much that I looked like a giant Q-Tip. I made the mistake of asking for a hand mirror. My long hair, usually tied in a ponytail or squished in a bun, would probably cover it.

I would have to wait and see about permanent brain damage but I thought I was processing things rather well then. I couldn't remember much, but again, that was 'normal.' Motor skills, too, would remain to be seen. At any rate, I would not be teaching for a while. I felt slightly affronted that my own city had harmed me.

Finally released from the hospital, with the proviso of follow ups with my doctor and physical therapy evaluations, I was given a clean bill of health. They were wrong.

I first noticed changes when I got home. I rent a tiny apartment in a building that used to be a hotel. A grand old dame she was with a dark lobby lined in faded red carpet. An ancient elevator creaked tenants to upper floors, but it was usually faster to take the stairs. I had a first floor studio with a window onto Yucca Street.

My across-the-hall neighbor had an interior studio with a garden view, which meant his window looked out onto a dirt lot and a 'garden' of weeds. It probably had been lovely in its day, but who knew? He also collected and dressed mannequins which decorated his one room and I found them extremely eerie. He, Chris, seemed nice, but the mannequin thing gave me reservations.

When I got home by taxi (the cops had towed my car from the bodega) I entered the apartment lobby and it was very bright. The manager had always kept it dark to save electricity but now it was lit by a glorious chandelier and the red carpet was actually covered in blue flowers with a wide gold border that I had never noticed before. Maybe he'd had it cleaned and wanted to show it off with better light? The lobby also smelled differently. It used to have a musty, old-lady smell, and now that was gone. Someone had done some cleaning.

I passed the elevator to reach my hallway just as it dinged and the doors opened. Well, the ding was new, too. A sophisticated-looking couple in some sort of period dress exited. Someone was having a costume party. A bit of money if they went to the effort to spruce up the lobby, too. It happened all the time in L.A.

A young man in a red uniform with two rows of gold buttons down the front and a round pill-box sort of hat held the door and smiled. We didn't have an elevator guy in our building, so he must be part of the party. Almost no one has a doorman or elevator guy. This is L.A., not New York.

My head hurt and I was tired. I headed down my own hall. The carpet was back to faded here. The familiar musty smell greeted me as I put my key in the lock. I dropped my stuff right inside the door and went straight to bed.

I dreamed of women in furs and men in fedoras dancing at a fancy supper club. The doorman was the clerk in the bodega.

I awoke to knocking and made my groggy way to the door. Through the peephole Chris' close-up eyeball met my gaze. That had been our tradition since we met a year ago.

"Hey, girl." Chris folded me in a hug when I opened the door.

"Hey, girl," I said back. Chris was an actor, but currently made a living as a drag queen. He did a pretty good Mae West, among others.

He pushed me away but held my shoulders. "Okay, lemme see it."

I complied by moving my hair and lifting the bandage so he could see the long line of black stiches knitting the scalp covering the gutter in the bone.

"Ohhh, that's gross."

"I know." I closed the door. "Tea?"

"Sure." He settled on my futon couch and pulled his aqua boa closer.

"Is that new?" I asked as I put the kettle on. "For the act?"

"Nope. Just took it off Lucy. I needed it more than she did today."

Chris named all his mannequins. Someday I would ask him how he got around his apartment without crashing into any of them.

"I like what they've done with the lobby." I got all the tea things and the water boiled.

"When did that happen? Party or something?"

"What do you mean?"

I brought the tea tray to the coffee table. "You know, did Rafael clean the carpets?" I referred to our building manager. "And I didn't even know there was a chandelier up there. It looks great. Smells so much better, too." I squeezed my tea bag out and set it on the saucer. Chris was still.

"What are you talking about? I know you got shot in the head, but seriously?"

Maybe Chris was yanking my chain. He wasn't much of a prankster, though.

Suddenly I felt unsure of myself and waited for Chris to smile or say, "gotcha!" He just pulled Lucy's boa closer and sipped his tea, eyeing me sideways.

"I guess I'm tired. Maybe my injury affects my perception or vision? I don't know. I was cleared to come home, but. . ."

My stomach flip flopped and my scalp prickled then burst into icy sweat. Chris scootched over and put a hairless arm around my shoulders.

"Maybe Rafael did do some work and I haven't noticed." He tried to soothe me. "You know I usually park on Wilcox and come in the other way.

We all had a back door key that opened what used to be the service entrance to the hotel. Since parking was always tight and the hotel had no lot or garage, we parked anywhere we could and came in that way instead of walking all the way around the building, almost a block, to the front. I was especially grateful when I came home late at night.

"Let's go see." He stood and held out his hand. "I want to see the chandelier."

I grabbed my apartment key and slid into the flip flops I keep by the door. The hall looked and smelled the same as it always did. We marched into the lobby area and I stopped. Dark, dreary, musty, and no chandelier. I looked closely at the carpet. I could barely see them but they were there—blue flowers and a dirty gold border, well, brown now.

The elevator stayed closed and dark. Something else I hadn't noticed. Our mailboxes. I never thought about them before, but when I came home from the hospital, I had seen not mailboxes, but cubbies for the rooms, messages, notes, bills. Those hotel pigeon holes had later been converted to receive tenants' mail. More than that, fronting the cubbies had been a long polished counter. A hotel lobby counter. And a man had stood behind it. I crossed to the mail boxes and saw the faded imprint of where the long ago counter had stood.

If I had imagined it, I had done an excellent job.

"You okay, hon?" Chris linked his arm through mine.

"I don't think so. I need to lie down."

Chris guided me back to my apartment. Sensing I wanted to be alone, he tucked me into bed. "I'll check on you later before I go to work. First show's at nine. Holler if you want anything."

"Thanks, Chris."

He let himself out but I didn't sleep. I went over every detail of what I'd seen. I didn't *feel* crazy, but maybe I'd move up the date of my check up.

I eventually drifted off and if Chris checked on me, I didn't hear him. I awoke when I turned over and the farm furrow in my head rebelled at the weight and insult.

I should plant carrots in there, I thought as I examined it in the bathroom mirror. I hadn't been allowed to get it wet so my hair was pretty gross. At the hospital they'd washed out only as much blood as they needed to treat me, and fortunately they hadn't cut or shaved a bunch more, but still. Ewww. I was sprouting some lovely colors as the facial bruises had risen to the surface and begun to turn like fall leaves. The darkest, around my eyes like a raccoon and spreading toward the hair, was where I face planted after getting shot. The bullet had spun me around and I didn't know if I'd hit the display rack or the floor first. Either way, I was surprised I didn't have a pork rinds package label tattooed there as well.

I was a horror, but I needed to get out into some fresh, brown, L.A. air. Maybe just a quick walk around the block. My occasional exit, my window, was not an option since it was about six feet off the street. I'd even come in this way once in a while, but jumping up in my condition was not going to happen. A quick, fond, memory of my friend Lisa and I returning late at night from listening to jazz and drinking *a lot* of wine out of a fish-shaped bottle. We staggered home and decided we were fine to come in through the window instead of going the extra block. We made it, but not without some Laurel and Hardy antics to shove one butt through the window, and then the other yanking on the arms. I truly don't remember which I did.

I got a Dodgers baseball hat and sunglasses and made my way to the street. A quick walk was out of the question, but a slow stagger was within the realm of possibility. I probably looked like the rest of the domicile-challenged in my crazy city. I made it most of the way before I felt done in. Starting to get dizzy and it had taken longer than I thought. It was also getting dark. Or maybe a storm was coming and cloud cover reduced the light. Whatever. I did not feel good at all. I reached the front and a doorman in regalia opened one huge glass door.

"Thank you," I said. He nodded and I was half way through the lobby when the smell and noise drew me up. Perfume, flowers, cigars. Lobby counter. Cubbies. Staff. Wow, it was bright. The chandelier was back and the carpets glowed. A few guests milled about or sat in club chairs sipping drinks. The men wore tailored suits and glossy shoes, the women had low-heeled shoes, long skirts and hats like little buckets. My head pounded and my scalp prickled like a swim cap of pins.

I froze and traffic milled around me. Could they see me? My hallucinations? A ding and the elevator doors opened, the same young man in the red suit, the uniform cousin of the doorman smiled at me.

"Hi," I said. More of a reflex than anything.

"Yes, ma'am. Going up?"

No, but maybe I would this time. "Sure. Thanks."

He had to notice I was oddly dressed and completely out of place. Maybe he was paid not to notice. This was no party. I stepped inside and the doors closed. I stared at him.

"Ma'am?"

"Yes?"

"What floor please?"

My building only had four floors, but maybe I wasn't even in my building anymore.

"The top, please."

"Yes, ma'am." He pressed a button and I noted that this building also only had four floors. That was something. This was going to be weird because I would have to ride the elevator back down since I had no business up there. The doors opened and I chickened out.

"Thank you, uh,"

"George," he supplied.

"Yes, George. I'm Maggie. Margaret."

He looked uncomfortable as the doors closed. I suppose the guests don't introduce themselves to the help in this place. Wherever it was. Is. Sheesh. I looked around but I had nowhere to go. This floor seemed as nice as the lobby, but darker. I sighed and pushed the down button.

"Weirdsville, here we come. Poor George." My head had resumed its throbbing and it covered the ding of the doors opening. Or I thought it did. A gust of urine scented air hit me and I stepped into my old crappy, smelly Hollywood elevator again.

Tears washed the back of my lids and the head pounding switched to the pin pricks. I didn't know whether to be scared of brain damage or a reaction to all the meds I was on. I had to get back to my apartment. I felt moderately safe there. Nothing changed when I came or went. Adrenaline cascaded down my spine. Which is worse? That it's all in my head? Or that it's somehow real.

I rushed back to my studio and locked the door. I let go and cried. Maybe time to call the doc.

* * *

Chris had sweetly helped arrange to get my car from the tow lot and I drove myself to the doctor's office. That appointment was a waste of time in that he pronounced me on the mend and within normal parameters. I almost laughed because I rearranged it to be 'paranormal' which seemed closer to the truth. At least I didn't have a tumor or swelling in my brain. But I still had my problem, but no name for it. I walked slowly up Yucca from my lucky parking spot toward the lobby. I was worn out from the trip and the earlier excitement. I just wanted to crash.

That was not to be. As soon as I touched the building door pull, my scalp prickled and the mild headache amped up to percussive throbbing. I had a feeling that I was not stepping into my apartment building, but into a thriving hotel lobby, circa 1920. I was sort of ready for it, so I tried to take in as many details as possible. I really enjoyed the fresh smell. People didn't seem to see me which seemed odd, because I could clearly see them. Experimenting, I approached the check-in counter.

"Excuse me," I said to the man poking slips into the guest pigeon holes. Nothing. I repeated it louder. Still nothing. A woman stepped up to the registry book, almost touching me. She did not notice I was there, even when I gently patted the fox stole she draped down her arm. It was gross and soft at the same time. Looked way too much like the animal and not much like a piece of clothing. Unless you lived in a cave.

Neither acknowledged me. The elevator remained closed, so I pressed the call button. At least George would talk to me. Maybe he'd know what was going on. The doors opened to reveal George slumped in a corner of the elevator, his pristine uniform now dark with blood.

"Oh, God!" I stepped inside. "George! George!" I felt for a pulse but didn't get one. "Help!" I yelled behind me. No one came. No one heard. The doors closed and the elevator rose, opening on the top floor where I'd been before.

An older couple, dressed to the nines, were deep in conversation. They stepped inside and stopped, seeing George on the floor. Neither looked at me as I still knelt beside him, holding his hand and trying to find his non-existent pulse.

"Oh, my," said the woman, tucking her head into her husband's chest.

"Holy mackerel," he added, pulling her close. The doors had shut and we began our descent to the lobby. They stayed as far from me and George as they could.

They bolted into the lobby the second the doors were wide enough to let them. I heard yelling as the man reported George. I knew there was no point in my saying anything so I just held George's hand. I don't know why. I guess I wished someone had done that for me when I'd been shot. I'd watched minutes of me all alone bleeding out on the bodega floor and knew no one had known or cared.

Eventually the cops came and pulled him out of the elevator. He'd been stabbed. No CSI here. About a million people came and went, watching George. From cops to guests, he was the show. If there was trace evidence it was long contaminated. No weapon under him when he was unceremoniously yanked out. I felt very sad. He'd been the only one to talk to me in this place.

Finally his body was taken away, but it didn't seem like folks cared a whole lot about him. I guessed I'd have to find out the next time I came into this time zone.

I headed to my own hallway and as soon as I turned the corner, I knew I was back in my building. Light from the windows facing Yucca St. streamed onto faded, filthy carpet. Head down, I reached my door. I put my key in the lock and saw Chris was next to me. I turned to tell him what I'd seen, but it wasn't Chris. It was George. In *my* time and place. I was more surprised than afraid. George wasn't scary while he was alive, and that hadn't changed when he died.

"Hi, George," was my brilliant, insightful greeting.

He smiled broadly. "Hey, you can see me. I wasn't sure about that."

"What's going on, George? This is a little weird." I remembered I was standing in the hall talking to nobody, so I moved inside. "Come on in." I invited him, just in case it was like vampires or something. Jeez, why did I have to think of that?

I held the door for him, probably completely unnecessarily, but my mama raised me right. "Is there anything you need?" I asked.

"Well, not in the way of hospitality, but it is nice of you to think of it."

He really had a lovely smile. His little pillbox hat still rode at a jaunty angle, the chin strap making his cheeks bulbous when he smiled. His uniform had several holes and the middle was completely maroon from the blood. I tore my eyes from his torso.

"It's okay, I'm kind of used to it being there now."

"Now?"

"You know, after so many years."

"Can you tell time I mean, not like a clock, but the passing of time?"

"Not really, but I can read. When our, shucks, how do I say it, uh, worlds cross, I can read your newspapers so I know what year it is."

"What year were you in?"

"1929."

"I am having information overload." I sat on my little futon. George floated in a sitting position slightly above the cushion next to me. "Why me? Why can you see me and no one else in the building could?"

"Maybe because I'm dead?"

"But I'm not dead."

"Yes, you are."

"What?" I thought I was going to heave.

"I'm sorry. You're not dead *now*. But you were. And that lets me talk to you."

"Oh, man." I got up and set the kettle on to make tea. Tea, my go-to cure for everything.

"Okay. How did I go back in time? To your time? Did you do that?"

"Nope. I was surprised as you to see you there."

"So I came to you." He nodded. "Well, I sure didn't plan to."

"Ghosts are attached to places or people, and maybe your attachment to the building let you in?" He was trying to be helpful. "I'm not even the only ghost there!"

He was so not being helpful. "How many of them are crawling around your building?"

"A few. One famous one, Victor Killian!"

My water boiled. I dunked a mint tea bag in my cup. Mint, good for nausea and headaches, of which I was having a lot lately. "Back to you. How are you in two places at once?"

"What do you mean?"

"You were there, in your time when I met you, and now you're here, in my time. Hey, can anyone see you now?"

"Probably not. No one could see you then but me. And thanks for holding my hand, by the way, that was nice. As to two places at once, I'm not really. You came back to me, in my time, so I was only there, then. You came to me. I didn't go anywhere. And now, I'm here with you." He smiled as if it all made great sense.

"Clears it right up," I muttered and threw my tea bag in the trash. I carried my cup back to the futon. "Let's just move on. So, why are you here? I understand that I somehow brought myself back to you, but why did I do it?"

"Maybe I called you? I didn't mean to, and I sure didn't know I could, but wouldn't that be nifty?"

"Yeah, nifty is the word. Why would you be calling?"

"I'm a ghost!"

"I know that. Clarify." His brow wrinkled. "I need more information. Why would you, or any ghost, call someone?"

"So we can stop being ghosts, of course."

"Of course." I sipped my scalding tea and thought. "You were murdered, right?"

"Yes." He stopped smiling. "It was strange and it hurt."

"I'm sorry. I want to figure this out. Did they ever solve your case? They didn't seem all that interested from what I could tell."

"Since I can't leave the building, I don't know, but I would guess not, since I'm still here."

"Okay." I sipped some more. "Maybe you need some help solving your murder? Do you think that's why you're sending out a virtual distress call?"

"I don't remember doing that."

"Never mind. Do you want to know what happened to you? Do you want to leave the building? Move on? Whatever you guys call it?"

"Oh, yes. My family must all be dead now, too. Wouldn't you think?" I nodded. "I'd love to see them again."

He looked so young. I forgot how young he must have been and his life had been cut short. I gathered my resolve.

"Okay. The first thing is we'll look it up on the internet."

"Neato! I love the internet!"

"How do you know about that?"

"I have nothing to do all day but wander around. Of course I pop into see what's going on. Everyone is on one of those book things." He pointed to my computer.

"It's called a laptop."

"Why? It's not on your lap."

"Good point.We'll call it a computer." He looked about to say something else so I cut him off. "It computes things, okay? How do you know about the internet but not what this is?"

"Everyone says they're going to search the internet, but no one says how they're going to do it. They don't say, I will get my laptop thing and search. They just do it."

"Fair enough."

He smiled happily as I scrolled through the choices the search box had given me. "Wow, this building is kinda famous," I mused as I clicked on various articles. "There's your buddy." I pointed to an article on actor Victor Killian's murder in 1979.

"He's not my buddy. He's kind of cranky. I'm nice to everyone. He could be, too."

"It is what it is." I clicked on an archived newspaper article from 1929. "What day did you die, do you know?"

"No, but I know the month. October. It was getting toward the end because the neighborhood had lots of Halloween decorations up."

"I should have asked this earlier, but I thought maybe you'd mention it. Do you remember who killed you?"

"Not who exactly, but I remember what happened." He shifted in his ghostly position on the futon.

"I'm sorry this is going to be hard. I need you to tell me about it. It doesn't have to be now, but sooner rather than later, if you want to get out of Dodge."

"Dodge?"

"You know like, Dodge City, in the old west?"

"Oh, yes. Dodge. I love western pictures."

For a second I didn't know what he was talking about until I remembered they called movies pictures, back in the day.

"Me, too. Do you think you can walk me through what happened?"

Even though he didn't need to breathe, in fact, I hadn't seen him take a breath the whole time we'd been talking, he gave a big sigh. Old habits die hard. And, it told me how hard this was for him. After what, like 90 years, you'd think it'd get easier. What did I know? I'd only been dead a little while and I didn't remember any of it.

"I was at work, like every other day. The hotel was full. I'd been really busy and gotten some good tips. A lot of times, no one tips me like they do a doorman or a porter, but today, people were really nice. I thought it was a good day."

"I'm sorry. Stay focused. Did anyone seem off to you? Strange? Threaten you?" I still clicked on links while I talked.

"No, nothing like that."

"Hey, look at this. Your murder is really close to the big stock market crash of October 29, 1929."

"Well, it happened after I died, so it's not like I caused it. Besides, that's New York and this is Los Angeles. They're a million miles apart."

"In some ways, yes, but in others not so much." I scanned an article. "There's a lot of info on the events leading up to the crash. How did people seem at the hotel? I mean the guests. This is a pretty posh place." I glanced at my peeling walls and water-stained ceiling. "Well, it was. Rich people were set to lose a lot of money. This article says people started pulling their money out. Lots of people bought on the margin—that means borrowing money to buy shares and only paying a small percentage of what the share is worth. There was even a 'mini-crash' in March of 1929."

"I don't remember much beyond the things I was able to show you."

"Okay. Lemme keep going. Well, there's certainly motive. Money is always motive, but it's not like you were a big investor. I wish I knew who was staying at the hotel then." My tea was cold but I drank it anyway. I felt I was close to something.

"'In the 1920s people borrowed a lot of money and used credit like never before,'" I read. "They got in trouble when market shares began to slip. Even JP Morgan tried to help by buying more shares to shore up reserves but that didn't work. People were scared so they tried to get their money out. Obviously, banks didn't have the cash and the stock market, which had been viewed like an 'ATM,'"

"What?" he interrupted.

"Cash machine. It's something more modern. It dispenses cash from your account instead of talking to a teller inside the bank." I'd lost him. "Never mind. Anyway, the banks and the stock market couldn't withstand the pressure of all those losses and collapsed."

"I think I remember people talking about financial instability. I wasn't dead yet, but they spoke about buying shares and money. One thing about being the elevator boy, is people treat you like you're invisible and just talk about their most private things! I remember this one lady telling her gentleman companion the most intimate—"

"Wait. What? People talked about this in front of you in the elevator?"

"Yes, I was so embarrassed." Even now he blushed at the memory. How does a ghost blush? A question for another time.

"Not that. Finances. Deals. People discussed that?"

"Sometimes."

"Think hard, George. This could be it. Think who was blabbing about that close to the time of your death. I might be able to verify it with hotel registry books if they still exist somewhere."

"Probably the basement." He was glum. "I don't remember. We had so many guests and so much coming and going. The only constant is the staff."

"Maybe one of them made a bad investment or something?"

"No one had money like that. And they didn't ride the elevator. They took the stairs. We're supposed to be invisible."

"Okay. Keep thinking while I read." I kept reading and scrolling. What a terrible time for the nation's finances and everyone's. The only thing I remember about that time was my mom telling me my grandfather wanted to buy houses right after the crash as an investment. Real estate would recover and he could have bought gorgeous homes for about $4000.00 each. But my grandma was too scared to spend the money and that's why we're not millionaires today. "Huh." I sat back and stretched my fingers. Nothing else, but I still felt I was close. I turned to George. He was very still. "What? Did you think of something?"

"A few days before I died the owner of the hotel visited. I thought it was strange because I'd never seen him before. We have a manager, well, a couple, and all of a sudden the owner was there." George closed his eyes, remembering. "He was taking around some people. . ." He opened his eyes wide. "I remember! He wanted to sell the hotel. He was from New York!"

"Are you sure about that? You're not making it up because of all the articles we've been reading? You said LA and New York are too far apart."

"I forgot. I'd never met the man until he started riding in my elevator." He closed his eyes again. "At first he was careful. He didn't say anything in front of me, but as the days passed, maybe he got used to me, or was worried about money. I know he was really interested in selling the building, and it seemed he knew there was a time factor."

"Really? Do you think that's possible? He knew something big was going to happen in the financial world?" I put in new search parameters. "Oh, my gosh! Someone knew. Roger Babson knew. He predicted it in a speech on

Sept. 5, 1929. It wasn't much of a secret if he said it to a room full of people." I read furiously.

"Well, most people didn't listen, I guess."

"Your hotel owner did. He sure wanted to liquidate the building and 'reef his sails' as Roger Babson said."

"He got out of Dodge, as you said." George smiled.

"Okay, really think George, back to those times the owner was in your elevator."

"Okay."

George was quiet for so long that I got up and made more tea and reheated the leftover chili Chris had made me.

"It's true. It was Mr. Greer, the hotel owner." George looked about to cry.

"Tell me what happened."

Again, George closed his eyes. He watched his private movie and recounted it for me. It happened the night before his death. Elliot Greer and a potential buyer had been in the elevator and Greer was showing him around. Greer spoke of this great investment and they rode to the fourth floor. As they got out, Greer's glasses fell out of his pocket onto the elevator floor. Not even George noticed them at the time. After going back to the lobby, he picked up a group and stopped at the second floor. A man leaving noticed the spectacles and handed them to George saying they didn't belong to anyone in this party.

George didn't know to which man they'd belonged and went back to the fourth floor and found only Greer talking on the phone. The door to the room was open and George clearly heard the plans of Elliot Greer to inflate the price of the hotel and its stock, swindle the buyer and skip town, cash in hand. It had to happen now. George heard Greer repeating the words of his rich New York friends. Now George was afraid and ran back down the hall to the elevator. He pushed the call button but not in time. Greer saw him step into the elevator and knew he'd heard too much.

"Who he thought I was going to tell is a mystery to me," George mumbled.

"I guess the idea of you telling anyone couldn't be risked. Maybe you died right before the crash, and that date was too close. If anyone speculated anything at all, that could have thrown a monkey wrench in the works and stalled the sale. If he really invested in this place, I mean I read it had only been completed the year before, he could lose everything."

"And the life of one nobody employee didn't matter next to his piles of money."

"I guess not." I reached out and took George's hand. For a second it wasn't even weird that I could do it.

"No good deed goes unpunished," George said.

"But it can be rewarded, even now. Let's look up Elliot Greer."

He brightened a little at that. A search revealed that Greer had indeed sold the hotel for quite a lot, even for back then. The sale closed on October 22, two days before the first crash, and a week before the second on October 29, 1929. Greer returned to his native New York only to be run over by a brand new Checker cab.

"Ha!" George was delighted.

I scanned some more. "It seems he left quite a mess behind. Wife, two daughters, a son, and a mountain of debt. They found a single ticket on him for a transatlantic ship to London. He was going to run!"

"Nuts!"

I looked at him sideways. "Nuts?"

"Well, I'm mad. He was going to get away with it. He did get away with it. My murder, I mean. And I'm stuck here."

"Oh. You don't feel a little, um, relieved?"

"I guess. But it's not justice and somehow I thought I could get justice. While we've been sitting here I was thinking how great it would be. You would find some descendent or something and tell all. Or that the interweb would have some article on how he lost everything."

"Interweb?"

"Yes, the world wide web. Isn't that what you call it?"

"Absolutely." I didn't have the heart to correct him. "You don't think that finding out the truth has 'released' you to move on?"

"I don't feel any different, really." He dropped his head. "I had such hope in you."

I tried not to take it personally. "Let's look you up. See if anything's been archived for you, okay?"

"Good idea."

"What's your full name and date of birth?"

"George Anthony Riddle. May 17, 1914."

"You were just a baby!"

"Old enough to have a job."

"That worked out well." I put in the information and nothing came up. Then I went to the public records of the county of Los Angeles and had better luck. A reference to a birth, not certificated since it was a home birth, but he existed. I followed a link to the LA Times which I was surprised to find was the newspaper way back then, just as now. The link was an article on his murder and ended with 'no suspects have been found and the murderer is still at large.' Another link took me to a follow-up article on cold cases twenty-five years later. Not a huge help, but I pointed out the section where they listed his next of kin. Although they'd all be dead now, it seemed to make him feel better. Maybe there's a search engine for ghosts in the ether that isn't the ethernet and he'd be able to find relatives more easily. I don't know. I don't want to know.

He heaved a big sigh.

I had to do something. "Since this didn't work, should we go to the scene of the crime? Maybe that will help. Come on." I stood and headed for the door. He walked through the wall.

We stopped facing closed elevator doors. It was my lobby, not his. That didn't seem helpful. I pushed the call button. When the car arrived, I stepped in but he hesitated.

"Come on. I'll be right here with you. It's not like you haven't ridden the elevator in 90 years." He still hesitated and I grabbed his hand and pulled him in. As soon as I touched him, the car shifted into the past. The walls were red flocked paper, the carpet matched the lobby: glossy blooms and gold border.

Something else happened. Elliot Greer and another man talked about the wonderfulness of buying the hotel. Another George stood at the ready, gloved hands clasped in front of him by the car buttons. We watched the glasses drop from Greer's pocket as they exited, the man going left, Greer going right. We rode the elevator back to the lobby and picked up a very happy group, one carried a gin fizz or whatever they drank back then. We still held hands, not only because I was terrified, but I knew if I let go, this blast from the past would end.

A man in the group picked up the glasses and handed them to Other George. It was surreal watching events unfold exactly as George had said, like actors following a script. I wish my memory was that good.

Other George rode back to four, and stepped down the hall to where Greer's phone conversation could be heard through the open door. Not very savvy of Greer, but I guess he was in panic mode. His words were more damning than George had thought and even as George hot-footed it in retreat, something made Greer go to the doorway and see a flash of red uniform and the elevator doors close.

It was worse than watching myself get shot. The next day, George took the elevator and Greer stepped in. It was over so fast.No discussion, no conversation. A shiny blur and George collapsed, bleeding. Greer stepped out of the elevator, back into his hall, completely clean and calm. Watching this I was a mess. I glanced at George and couldn't read his face. Sadness, yes, maybe some satisfaction. I don't know.

"Oh, George! I'm so sorry. This is terrible." I turned to hug him and the moment I let go, he began to fade.

"I can go now. I can tell. Thank you so much for all your help. All you did."

"Wait, George! Don't go yet. I still have questions!"

"I might see you again. Who knows? And we both know you can do extraordinary things, Margaret."

The elevator closed once again and it descended to the lobby. I didn't know how to feel. I hardly knew George but I felt like I'd lost a friend. Did he find justice? Maybe not, but I guess he found satisfaction. No, peace. I think that's what I saw on his face at the end. Peace. He'd let it go so he could move on. Tears started to well as the elevator hit the lobby and the doors opened.

A figure waited there. "It's about time. Now it's my turn. Well, you're pretty foxy, so we're going to be groovy together," said Victor Killian's ghost.

Judythe Guarnera

Judythe Guarnera, editor of the "nightwriter" co
lumn in Tolosa Press for five years and the editor of the
SLO NightWriter Anthology, has been published in local
publications and in six anthologies (including *Chicken Soup
for the Soul*). She has been a frequent winner in the Lillian
Dean Contest at the Central Coast Writers Conference and a
finalist in the NW Golden Quill Contest. She is a Mentor
Mediator, which gives her more opportunity to connect, as
she does through her writing.

Judythe is inspired by the number of
women who face their very real fears with courage and
humor, as does her protagonist in *Digging Deep for Courage*.

DIGGING DEEP FOR COURAGE
by
Judythe Guarnera

The entire day had seemed out of kilter—nothing
really wrong, but not right, either. Living on California's

Central Coast had been a dream come true, so I resented even a single lovely day laced with tension.

I arrived home at twilight. Before I could put my key in the front door-lock, a movement in the bushes caught my eye.

I'd been one of those cautious kids who always had to look in the closet and under the bed before I could go to sleep. And after what happened last year . . .

No surprise that I shifted into defense mode. Despite the menacing shadows scattered everywhere and the fact that my shoulders ached from the weight of the fear I carried, I charged forward.

My eyes swiveled like a praying mantis with its two sets of eyes. I held my keys out, ready to jab any intruder who got in my way. I checked the bushes, even lifting fronds and peering underneath. The hairs on my neck stayed at attention even though I found nothing, not even my cat.

Once inside, I double-locked all the doors. I turned on the recessed lighting under the kitchen cupboards and a table lamp next to the bed. Room by room, I checked every crevice and corner. Nothing and still no sign of my cat. *She probably slipped out while I was busy being paranoid.* I thought about leaving the back door open for her, but I was too scared. She'd be okay; her middle name could be independence. Mine could be chicken.

I kicked off my shoes, poured myself a glass of Chardonnay and carried it into the bathroom. I resisted the impulse to gulp it down, and sipped as I walked. I set it on the counter.

As part of my recovery, I had tapped into my funky sense of style and filled my bathroom with Betty Boop memorabilia. The red, white, and black polka-dot pattern of the wallpaper continued the theme. Believe me, the room looks, feels, and even smells cheerful. To this day, it lifts my spirits. One more sip of the woody Chardonnay and I almost forgot how scared I'd been not fifteen minutes earlier.

I love to sing in the shower—the louder, the better—in this sacrosanct spot where no one can hear my off-tune renditions. I turned on the faucet, let the water warm up and eased in. *Aah!* I lathered my hair, piled it on top of my head and sucked in a lungful of air, ready to belt out the first verse of "Singing in the Rain," when I heard a muffled sound.

I froze, literally and figuratively, shampoo running into my eyes. I stabbed at the suds. "Dang!" My hot water heater must have given up the ghost. *Oops. Poor choice of words.* I stepped away from the cold water.

I took a breath and let my body calm down so I could focus on listening. Nothing. The sound of nothing continued until I relaxed again. *Get a hold of yourself, girl.*

I needed to rinse my hair, so I braced myself as I moved under the cold water, only to discover it was warm again. *That's weird.*

Thud.

Now every iota of my being was focused on one thought—intruder/rapist. There was definitely someone in my bedroom and he was getting closer.

Oh no, not again. No, God, no, please! It can't happen again.

I slid to the floor, the memory of the rape, not even a year ago, so vivid I could feel the pain of his arm taut around my neck, his gloved hand over my mouth. Déjà vu permeated the air, clogged my lungs. My gut tightened.

Just as I began the plunge into helplessness, from somewhere deep inside me, I heard, "*Stop it!*" After a year of therapy and finally able to see myself as a survivor, not a victim, I was just going to give up? *No way!* I looked up to see Betty Boop, hands on hips, staring down at me from the ceiling.

I elbowed myself to a sitting position and pulled my body upright. The water was cold again. *Looney Tunes time or maybe Twilight Theater.* I took a deep breath.

I turned the shower head, water still running, toward the back wall. Best to let the intruder think I was still unaware of his presence.

A weapon; I needed a weapon. I grabbed the spray bottle of Tilex from the rack under the shower head and rotated the nozzle to the on position. *Let's see how he likes a face full of bleach.*

Not much protection, but it'd buy me time. Once the bastard was out of commission, I'd grab my robe and beat it out the front door and head for my neighbors—the big football players next door.

I forced myself to listen for more unwelcome sounds. Nothing. It was quieter than a cemetery covered in snow on a winter night. Could it have been my overactive imagination—all the residual fear from the other break-in?

Another distinct sound of movement dispelled that notion. Should I just stay in here and wait? *Wait for what—to be a victim again?* The hot water had disappeared and my nakedness definitely added to my sense of vulnerability.

As I gathered my courage around me like the bathrobe I wished I was wearing, I stepped back in time for a moment, remembering when I was ten. My parents were out. I heard a noise in my closet and I ran to get my brother. When he opened the closet door, a tiny brown mouse scampered out and disappeared down the hall. I refused to be that scared little girl again.

A gentle push on the shower door allowed me enough room to squeeze through. I reached for my cell. I always put it on the counter, but not this time. Probably still in my purse. When I get scared, my brain turns to mush and routine flies out the window.

I inched open the bathroom door with my left hand, the right clutching the Tilex bottle, and peered into the bedroom. Across the widening space, the bed lamp cast shadows, shadows that might harbor the intruder.

My eyes popped when I saw a pile of broken pottery, clumps of dirt and my battered Schefflera plant, center stage on the Oriental rug. I lowered my weapon—I mean my spray bottle. A movement on the bed drew my gaze.

Medusa, my calico cat, took a breather from the task of licking dirt from her paws and gave me one of her 'What's your problem?' looks. My legs gave out and I sat with a thump on the floor. Medusa curled up in my lap.

Little minx had been out to get that plant since the day I brought it home.

AUTHOR SHOWCASE

As all authors, we love to hear from our readers. Here's how to contact the writers in this volume, and how to find their other works.

1. Diane Boyles: website: dianebroyles.com

   a.Kris Lynn: email: krislynn.writer@gmail.com; Website: www.kristalynn.com; Twitter: KristaWriter; Facebook Writers Page: www.facebook.com/KristaLynnWrites; Amazon Author Page: www.amazon.com/-/e/ B01CXFM3S

2. Paul Alan Fahey: Website: http:// pualalanfahey.com; email: paulfa1189@gmail.com; Goodreads blog: www.goodreads.com/author/show/ 6452410.Paul_Alan_Fahey/blog

3. Judythe Guarnera: Contact Judy through email: j.guarnera@sbcglobal.net, or Facebook: JudytheGuarnera

4. Victoria Heckman: Visit her website: www.victoriahekman.com; find her on Facebook, Twitter and Instagram

5. Paul Alan Fahey: email: paulfa1189@gmail.com; website: http://paulalanfahey.com; Goodreads blog: goodreads.com/author/show/6452410.Paul_Alan_Fahey/blog

6. Mary Moses: email: mjmoses9922@gmail.com

7. Janice Konstantinidis: email: jkon50@gmail.com

8. Lani Steele: Facebook: Dr.LoniSteele

9. Dianne Emley: Website: www.DianneEmley.com; Facebook: DianneEmleyAuthor; Twitter: DianneEmley; Goodreads.com/author/show/83073.Dianne_Emley

10. JoAnne Lucas: jlucas3465@att.net

11. Susan Tuttle: Website/blog: www.SusanTuttleWrites.com; Facebook: susanwriter; Twitter: @STuttleWriter; LinkedIn; Goodreads.